– 2 –

YASEMIN'S STRUGGLE

One voice among thousands

Nurgül Sönmez

FSC
www.fsc.org

MIX

Papier aus ver-
antwortungsvollen
Quellen
Paper from
responsible sources

FSC® C105338

Bibliografische Information der Deutschen Nationalbibliothek: Die Deutsche
Nationalbibliothek verzeichnet diese Publikation in der Deutschen Nationalbibliografie;
detaillierte bibliografische Daten sind im Internet über http://dnb.dnb.de abrufbar.

Die automatisierte Analyse des Werkes, um daraus Informationen insbesondere
über Muster, Trends und Korrelationen gemäß §44b UrhG (Text und Data Mining")
zu gewinnen, ist untersagt.

© 2021 Nurgül Sönmez

Lektorat: Ömer Faruk Arslan
Korrektorat: Berna Arslan - Arzu Kaya
Weitere Mitwirkende: Gamze Taşdemir

Verlag: BoD · Books on Demand GmbH, Überseering 33, 22297 Hamburg,
bod@bod.de
Druck: Libri Plureos GmbH, Friedensallee 273, 22763 Hamburg

ISBN: 978-3-7693-0866-2

Imprint

YASEMIN'S STRUGGLE – 2

Originally translated from German, published in 2022 ©

Nurgül Sönmez

Translation: Nurgül Sönmez
Compilation / Editor: Ömer Faruk Arslan
Proofreading : Berna Arslan
Final Check : Arzu Kaya
Book Cover Design: Gamze Taşdemir
Illustration / Index: Gamze Taşdemir

Author Contact Information:

✉ ns.nurgulsonmez@gmail.com
🅕 nurgulsonmez
🅞 nurgulsonmezofficial

Team:

g.tsdmrr@gmail.com

nurgulsonmezofficial

nurgulsonmez

To all book lovers...

Biography

Nurgül Sönmez

21.08.1979
Germany

In the years between 1995-2020, she often received awards.
She began writing in 1995 and has written countless poems,
song lyrics and novels. Written based on true events.
The rights to over 50 novels and over 2500 song lyrics were taken over
by various publishers and famous composers.
Now she no longer stands behind the scenes,
but with her works in the middle of the stage.

Nurgül Sönmez
– Schriftstellerin –

AUTHOR'S WORKS

- Her first book ANA (Poem - Turkish) was published in **2014**
- **2015** YASEMİN'İN SAVAŞI (Turkish)
- **2017** YASEMİN'İN İNTİKAMI (Turkish)

2021

- Matilda (Turkish, German)
- 1001 GECE YERİNE - BİN BİR GÜN (Turkish)
- STATT 1001 NACHT - TAUSENDUNDEIN TAG (German)
- YASEMİN'İN ÇARESİZLİĞİ 1 (Turkish)
- YASEMİN'İN SAVAŞI 2 (Turkish)
- YASEMİN'İN İNTİKAMI 3 (Turkish)

2022

- Matilda (English)
- YASEMINS VERZWEIFELUNG 1 (German)
- MAAROUF (Turkish, German)
- INSTEAD OF 1001 NIGHT - THOUSAND AND ONE DAY (English)
- YASEMINS KAMPF 2 (German)

2023

- YASEMINS RACHE 3 (German)

2024

- YASEMIN'S DESPERATION 1 (English)
- YASEMIN'S STRUGGLE 2 (English)
- YASEMIN'S REVENGE 3 (English)
- MAAROUF (English)

All books have been translated into French and are planned for future book projects. This will be followed by translations into Arabic and Spanish. If there is interest and demand, there will also be translation in other languages.

Her works © are based on true events and she continue to support social projects with the proceeds of the books.

Soon also available as audiobooks!

Nurgül Sönmez
– Schriftstellerin –

Thousands of voices can be hope for a voice.

Based on a true story!

Struggle!

Yasemin goes to a foreign country in complete sadness.
She is not familiar with either the culture or the language.
Pain does not stay away for long on this journey either.

Nevertheless, she firmly believes that she will not give up.
Determined and full of courage, her struggle begins.

A struggle that will demand everything from her.

Will she be able to protect herself and her siblings?

Will she gain the victory?

CHAPTER
1

My Beloved Home!

An iron gate opened automatically in front of us. The driver drove slowly through it. Suat cried out in astonishment, smiling and surprised. "Oh, what a beautiful sight! What a beautiful place it is." Yes, it really was, it was a beautiful place.

When we wanted to take our luggage with us, the master of the house said: "What are you doing there? Let go. Your luggage will be brought in." Then he smiled again as he turned to me and said, "I would be happier if you just said Hikmet, my child." They were very warm, just hearing that was enough for me. "Did my wife Filiz tell you about our daily routine on the way?" He asked.

"Yes, she did. You have thought very carefully. It will do us all good if family friends come to visit."

I was determined to share my experience, but it was also important that we build trust and sympathy for one another. In fact, the excitement was great. If I couldn't get close to the family, I would be silent and unable to speak. I said to myself, "I hope we will be compatible"

Then Hikmet, the master of the house and his honored wife Filiz, the lady of the house, showed us the whole house and the surroundings.

Don't look at me when I called it home, this was a very, very luxurious villa. Access was through a large iron gate. The total area was seventeen thousand, even more seventeen thousand five hundred square meters. The entrance was fitted with a private security booth and camera systems showing the entire area. Black-clad security guards were also active. After walking a long way through the big and wide grassland, the villa appeared right in front of us in all its glory. It had a mesmerizing beauty with its seating, the paradise garden of colorful flowers and plants that gave people tranquility just by watching. The terrace alone lay in front of our feet in all its beauty. The presence of a large swimming pool was like the name of the fun that made the summer months the chilliest of days. A large piece of land was set aside for three beautiful horses and paddocks. A little further there was a beautiful outbuilding, carefully built for the staff and thought out to the smallest detail.

The villa itself had eight parking spaces, four of which were open and four covered. The exterior of the villa was magnificent as was the garden area. It was immaculate and partially decorated with white and cream colored tesserae. Modern lanterns provided sufficient light. Inside, I couldn't hide my surprise when I found a large living room, two kitchens, a bathroom and a toilet, an indoor floor-to-ceiling pool area and a Turkish bath.

As soon as I saw the rather large and ornate dining table, the first thing that came to my mind was that it was the area where crowded meetings were held and crowds of guests received. One of the kitchens was set up like a restaurant kitchen as you know it. It has been meticulously thought out down to the last detail. All the preparations for the special guests have been carefully made in this kitchen. The other kitchen was very stylish with white high gloss furniture where the daily meals were prepared. There was a separate door for staff to enter the kitchen. There was also a special area built just for them. Paintings carefully made by Filiz hung on almost every wall of the object.

As I climbed the stairs, with every step I saw more pictures of Filiz stylishly adorning the walls. Upstairs were the rooms for my siblings and me. My room had an en-suite bathroom while my siblings had separate rooms and a shared bathroom area. The rooms of the couple Hikmet and Filiz were on the upper floor. There was also a large cinema. Everything was very luxurious.

However, I had seen worldly possessions but not worshiped them. I had experienced both wealth and poverty but God is the giver and the taker.

Peace, love and affection reigned throughout the house. All the beauties caressed my soul.

The staff brought us all lemonade. It was the first time I was treated like a child. I never knew that feeling. Because I had always faced older, more mature behavior. Everyone had higher expectations due to my age and for the first time I was a kid here. The first time! It felt good, I couldn't describe how good it was.

Hikmet and his wife Filiz introduced us to the house staff. The gardener Osman was married to Aunt Meral. The couple were responsible for the family and the staff. The personal driver of the family was called Ahmet. In the case of crowded parties and dinners, special chauffeurs were brought in to transport the guests. Hasan was the head chef of the house and two other chefs worked with him. Dilek and Elif were responsible for the housework. Uncle Osman and Aunt Meral managed all the staff and other family concerns. There were also three other household helpers: Natalia, Filiz and Selda. That day we met Uncle Osman, Aunt Meral, Dilek and Selda for the first time.

It was like paradise here. The peaceful nature was reflected on my face. When Suat saw his teacher Nihat coming, he called out, "My teacher is coming." He got up happily. Suddenly, teacher took the tray from the staff and brought it to us himself. What a surprise! "The drinks have come. The services are mine", he said cheerfully, putting a smile on everyone's faces.

After serving the drinks, Suat's teacher first greeted Hikmet: "My dear father!" When he saw his son and he kissed his hand, his eyes shone. He was his pride and joy. He let this feeling be felt in every respect. He stroked his hair with one hand. "Welcome, son," he greeted affectionately.

Then it was his mother's turn, whom he kissed on an elegant level, saying, "My Queen, dear mother." But he didn't put her hand on his forehead, which was the first time I saw someone's hands like that to kiss. What a polite treatment.

His mother was also enchanted by him. "My son, my child, my only son. My eyes were already looking for you. Welcome home," she said with a warm smile. At that moment I saw on Suat's face, sadness, his chin was shaking slightly and his eyes were filled with tears. I immediately understood my brother's condition. At that time, his teacher immediately turned to Suat, who had also seen the tears: "Suat, welcome!" He kissed his cheeks and then hugged him warmly. "Yasemin, my dear sister, you are also very welcome! " he added, kissing my cheeks and hugging me like a loving brother. He seemed even kinder to his family. But such bad things had happened that it wasn't even possible to be warm and sincere. Finally, he turned to Kiraz, whom he also hugged and kissed.

Together we sat down at the table, where he got down to business without breathing: "Father, mother, I have to talk to you about a very important topic about Yasemin. I'm leaving tomorrow morning, but first we need to discuss this matter. If necessary, we must intervene immediately." Without wanting to be disrespectful, I directly involved: "But not in front of my siblings, definitely not." Everyone had agreed with my decision. Suat's teacher spoke up again, "Then let's get up and talk in another room. " He was already getting up, but Filiz, amazed at his reaction, protested. "Son, let the children breathe. Then we go and talk. Is it that urgent What's going on here? "

"Mother, father. It's more urgent than we think, let's go in please, we have to intervene immediately if necessary," said Nihat.

Thereupon everyone got up immediately without further contradicting. In one room we took our seats in armchairs. My brother Nihat related what he had seen and heard. There were good things and bad things. As he looked more closely at the marks of the beating on my face, he became even more angry. "Yasemin, tell us what happened. You don't have to tell everything. Just tell us what you can, you're safe here. Absolutely nothing will happen to you, you can be sure of that." He challenged me. Filiz and Hikmet kept looking at each other. "What's going on here?" the question was reflected in their expression.

I respected all three very much. With all my courage I could say it on the phone, but now, sitting across from them, greeted so kindly and warmly, I couldn't pollute their lives and their views on us with these nightmares and traitors. I started to cry. No, I couldn't tell. It felt like I had swallowed my tongue. As Filiz got up and hugged me, resting my head on her shoulder and running a hand over my hair, Nihat began to speak:

"Yasemin, my beautiful sister. It's not your fault, you know that. I see you, you don't have to be afraid of us, we are your family. I know it's hard to tell, it's not easy. But I must now say it with mercy."

I could live with that, I nodded, but I couldn't stop crying. I hid my face in shame.

Before Nihat began to speak, Hikmet suddenly took over in his full wisdom: "Nihat, was Yasemin raped?" He had asked clearly. "Yes, my father. I gave her to her aunt yesterday with my own hands. There were no signs of beatings on her face. She was abused and beaten by her aunt this morning. When her aunt went to the market, her brother-in-law raped her," he confirmed.

Sobs came over my mouth. My head was still resting on Filiz's shoulder. His father took immediate action. "Darling, don't leave her, stay with Yasemin. I will inform my friends (doctor, inspector, commissioner, prosecutor, etc.) that we are coming. Everything necessary is initiated immediately. We're leaving now, get ready. We don't have a minute to lose." He instructed, then got up to call his office. After Filiz helped me wash my face, we walked to the car together.

"What will happen now?" I asked Filiz anxiously.

"Don't worry, my daughter, we'll go to the clinic first. You will be treated in order to be able to file a criminal complaint with the public prosecutor's office, we need a medical report. This phase may be exhausting for all of us, but we will get through it together. Happy days await us, my dear Yasemin."

All my worries and fears were gradually taken away from me.

After my health check was over, hormone injection therapy was done to keep me from getting pregnant. I didn't know the exact name yet. But later I found out that there is a cure to not get pregnant. It is given for three days. The commissioner, a friend of the master of the house and Hikmet, came to the hospital with three police officers. Only the professor and I were in the doctor's room. The others waited at the door. They came to the hospital so we wouldn't waste time. So I related what had happened.

All of a sudden, the inspector said. "That's enough for now, little one." The words stuck in my throat as I made my statement. Most of what I wanted to say didn't come off my lips.

After the first statement, they explained to me that they could arrest him immediately and bring him before the prosecutor's office and that after the hospital we had to go to the police station. Meanwhile, they arrested my brother-in-law.

As I related this, what my father had done to me at the police station flashed before my eyes like a film strip. It was my own father who subjected me to this cruelty, who prevented me from testifying. Who had prevented the punishment of those who had wronged his own daughter and ruined his daughter's reputation.

This time, the rapprochement of a family I had never known before with such optimism and warmth brought me to justice. What mattered was humanity, it was priceless. Either she was in the hearts or she wasn't. This was the love of God. In this company I felt safe again from the heart. With their honesty, faith, conscientiousness and that compassion in their beautiful hearts.

On the way from the hospital to the car, Filiz said. "My dear Yasemin, now Hikmet and his friend the commissioner will receive the arrest warrant from the prosecutor's office. The person who did bad things to you will be arrested.

The driver will now drop us off at the police station. Our lawyer is there, I have also informed my friend, the psychiatrist. It would be better for you if you gave your testimony before the commissioner and the judge in the presence of a lawyer and a psychiatrist."

Suddenly I felt a sense of relief, I was facing a first I had never experienced before. This time it was a fight for me, they would listen to me and appreciate me. So this is family love! So that's called family love!

At the police station we were treated very well. They immediately took us to the commissioner's room and served us tea, water etc. The psychiatrist, Nalân, seemed to me to be very warm, too. Her approach was very sincere and loving. At that moment I decided to talk to her. At the same time, I listened to what the lawyer was saying to Filiz. They were formal but also sincere as they were also family friends.

Then Filiz came to me and hugged me. "My dear Yasemin, my little rose," she said in a reliable and sincere tone, kissing the top of my head. "Everything will be fine, believe me." Though it was hard for me to believe, I sighed "God willing."

The commissioner and Hikmet had also arrived at the police station. Before they entered the room, a voice called out in the hallway. 'No one leaves the room until the commissioner arrives,' said Mr. Mustafa, the lawyer. I suddenly felt a little nervous about everything. We were all excited.

Hikmet wondered at me: "We are with you, my little one, don't be afraid!" He stroked my hair tenderly.

"I'm not scared anymore. You've given me so much confidence that I'm no longer afraid." I replied.

While I was giving my testimony in a casual and difficult manner, only the lawyer, the psychiatrist and the detective were in the office. Hikmet, Nihat and Filiz were housed in another room because they didn't want to face the crime family face to face.

My brother-in-law was arrested. The inspector persuaded him: "You will soon be brought before the magistrate. Be sincere! They will face you to the criminal. The magistrate will ask you important questions. You must answer these questions." Then the inspector turned to me: "We have your medical reports. You will also be present at the magistrate. If you cannot speak, remember that the lawyer and the psychiatrist are with you. You don't need to be scared. The law is behind you. This is a democratic country, nobody can harm you, nobody can oppress you. You have rights."

Of course I was excited. For the first time, people stood behind me. Those who did harm would suffer their punishment in this world and in the hereafter. A voice called me from the corridor to the magistrate. He wanted to take my statement and asked me to come in alone. My file was in front of him, and he quickly scanned the pages. I didn't know how to act. Then he started questioning us. Of course there were questions that I found difficult. It took me a while to answer and I swallowed hard.

Realizing I was having trouble telling the whole story, I asked permission for my psychiatrist and attorney to enter the room. After agreeing, they were brought in. Not wanting to testify in the same room as my brother-in-law, I was relieved to have assistance.

After I gave my testimony, my attorney told the magistrate. "We will submit the written statement to you again so that nothing is missing from your testimony." Hikmet, Filiz, the attorney, the psychiatrist, and I were able to leave after we gave the statement had signed.

I was tired. The whole thing had exhausted me. That feeling was relieving, as if the burden had been lifted from me. The odds were good.

What would happen now?

What would I experience next?

I didn't know. This uncertainty was like a heavy burden for me. While Filiz held my shoulder with one hand, Hikmet on the other hand gave me a lot of confidence. I felt sadness and heaviness. The driver brought the car to the gate of the police station, opened the doors and waited for us. I went step by step into an unknown life.

"Everything is fine" will forever remain my favorite lie. Because everyone believes in them, and I don't have to explain anything.

Yasemin's Struggle

CHAPTER
2

While Hikmet was away, he called the house and asked Suat and Kiraz to prepare. "We're coming to pick up the kids," he said, and hung up.

Then he called a restaurant and reserved a table. "Keep the next tables free, I need quiet," he asked. At that moment I looked confused at Filiz. She just smiled and stroked my hair.

He then called Eda, his private chief secretary, who he instructed that even the children's boutique should be closed.

"Were they that rich?" the thought crossed my mind. What we wanted wasn't clothing or garment, we just wanted a normal life and being able to be children. A life under normal conditions, nothing more.

To Hikmet and Filiz, who wanted to give us the best of everything, I said in embarrassment. "Please, please, you embarrass me enough as it is. You have done more than necessary. There is no need for what you are doing now. We don't want that much from you! Like a mother and like a father, you opened your arms and the door of your house to us. You supported us I can't ask for more from you. Please, I'm embarrassed."

"Don't worry, my child. Everything is as it should be. After picking up Suat and Kiraz, we go shopping and then we go to dinner. We have enough for today. Tomorrow we will all wake up to a new day together. I hope a new day awaits us. Afterwards we will talk about school and the daily routine so that we can put your life in order. " Hikmet and Filiz kissed my forehead warmly.

It was the first time I had tasted so much love, respect, appreciation, trust and safety. What a comforting feeling it was to have a family and to feel wings from a guardian angel. I fell in love with both of them at first sight. They were warm and sincere. The peace of being in secure welled up in me. It was a warm feeling, very warm...

At the house, the children were standing in front of the garage. Nihat offered: "I will follow you with Suat and Kiraz and give you moral support."

Without wasting any time, we continued on our way. The tiredness of the day weighed on me. The weight of the painful memories I had experienced crushed me. In the car, I leaned on Filiz's shoulder. I was mentally and physically tired. I didn't want to go anywhere or do anything but we were all hungry. I didn't want to spoil and upset their plans. According to them, they had dreams for us that they wanted to make come true. I was afraid that if I objected or tried to prevent it, I might hurt them.

First we went shopping. They closed the boutique for us and dressed my siblings from head to toe. I wasn't used to this luxury. Every time I got my hands on something, I gave it to my siblings.

Filiz understood me. "We'll come back here with you. It's been a very emotional day for you," she said. Luckily they had my siblings fully equipped. It was the first time I had seen them so happy in days. After shopping we went to the restaurant. I had never eaten at a table like this before. I was always afraid of doing something wrong. They ate with fine cutlery, I had never learned or seen eating with a knife and fork! They deprived us of everything that would await us in the new life. I said "Hello!" to a life I was getting to know for the first time! It was a loving life that gave us safety and security. First of all we said hello to the life that will lead us to live our childhood. When we got home that day, I was very tired. Filiz was almost like an angel with wings around me to take care of me. She could understand my physical and mental exhaustion.

Yasemin had sent me these words in a voice recording. The recording she made filled the entire tape, which I listened from start to finish. I almost fell into the tape, so excited.

When I got to the end, I called Yasemin to congratulate her. She deserved praise for her courage, determination, warrior spirit, productivity and decency. On the phone she then told me that she had also started to make an audio recording with the third cassette. Of course I was very happy about this news.

The entrance especially "HOW" Yasemin entered my private life was different from the other people I had met in life. She had left marks on me. "I'm glad she's one of those rare people I consider valuable."

Almost two weeks had already passed. There was no trace of the third recording that Yasemin had started. We had hardly spoken on the phone in the last few days because we both worked very hard and under difficult conditions. The ability to capture their experiences also depended on their emotional focus. In fact, it was well into the third week before Yasemin's cassette reached me. It evoked the same excitement and emotion as the first cassette I received. I wanted to end the shift and listen to the recording. Yasemin continued them as follows:

Filiz came into the room with me and kept assuring me: "This is your home now, my dear Yasemin, my beautiful daughter, everything will be all right. Even if today is our first day, look how positive it went." In fact, she was right. From this family I experienced the love, care, warmth, value, respect and importance that I had not even seen from my own family.

She had filled the tub for me and was doing her best for me to rest. As she took care of my siblings, the tiredness of the day in the bathtub eased.

From time to time I felt like screaming as much as I could. I could have gotten over what I had been through in one fell swoop. But I couldn't scream through the walls imbued with a sense of peace and security. If I wanted to, they would definitely let me. As long as I got back to myself as soon as possible. I was pretty sure of that.

After a nice and relaxing bubble bath, I dried my hair, then I entered my siblings' room. Filiz read a fairy tale to my siblings. I slowly approached them when she gave me a coming signal with one hand. She quietly opened the covers, I was surprised because I hadn't expected this. Overjoyed, I crawled under the covers. I couldn't describe how beautiful it was. I think it was the best memory I had after those nightmare filled days, as well as those beautiful, fine people I met.

Under the blanket, Suat had fallen asleep on Filiz's left side. Kiraz and I lay on the right side. With her left hand Filiz held the book, her right hand took it from Suat put it on my head and stroked my hair instead of Kiraz, my hair. It was like feeling an angel's wing and a mother's arm. I would never trade that feeling even if they gave me millions. Some time ago I wanted to scream as loud as I could, but now I lay quietly on the bed listening to a fairy tale.

There are people who love you and
people who love what they do for them.
Know the difference.

CHAPTER
3

When I woke up in the morning, I was alone in bed. My siblings and Filiz were no longer in the room. Suddenly I was alarmed. I immediately ran into the room assigned to me, changed my clothes and hurried to the first floor. I didn't know what time it was. When I found her eating breakfast, I was relieved. I didn't know myself like that. As I approached the table, I apologized to everyone for my lateness. In fact, I was always one of the first to wake up and prepare the breakfast table, but everyone understood.

The day's program was discussed at the table. It was mentioned that Suat and I should be enrolled in a private school. I was amazed at that, they wanted to enroll me in school again. I couldn't understand that. I never imagined that the topic of a hopeful future, the dream of which has already been taken from me, would take place at this breakfast table. The dream of going to school was shattered, I had never achieved it, hadn't even been there.

Surprised but polite, I interrupted the conversation when the subject of Suat's school came up: "Yes, my brother Suat shouldn't miss school. He should be registered at school. I can work and pay the school fees myself. "

"Well, if you work, how do you go to school?" Hikmet asked.

This question remained unanswered. "We will register you at school, Yasemin. You too will start school again. A bright and healthy future awaits you all," he then said.

I froze at the table in surprise for a moment. Of course, deep down, I want to learn as much as possible, but how? I wasn't ready yet. Besides, that dream had already been taken from me. The joy and hope of going to school had been lost. My wounds were so deep that I was distracted with sighs at the table, wondering how can I go to school with these wounds.

Besides, Kiraz was small. Who will take care of her when I went to school? I hesitantly shared what was on my mind with my family members. I explained my concerns and fears, but I also shared my love for school and my dream that was taken away from me. Above all, I said that I was no longer a little girl and took responsibility for my siblings.

In his gentle, compassionate, and dependable voice, Hikmet soothed me. "Have no worries or fears. Yesterday Filiz spoke to our therapist friend, Ms. Nalân. You can go to your sessions after school and continue your treatments. Your wounds will heal day by day. Remember that my Lord who bears the burden also gives the remedy. God does not give anyone a burden that they cannot bear. It is God who gives the healing. First of all we will thank him. We will pray and hope. If He wills anything will happen when He says not even a leaf falls from the tree unless He wills it. Not all good can be considered good, not all evil can be considered evil. Therefore, let us always ask for the best of our Lord, and whatever is best, may my Lord grant it to us. Kiraz is four years old and Filiz is also working. We enroll Kiraz in kindergarten. There she learns to share with other children, to play, to take a step into social life. We go to Suat's school, discover his talent and introduce him there. Whether music, art, sport, knowledge or whatever. We put our power into empowering and supporting the talent and skills of everyone, wherever they are. That goes for Kiraz and you too. Look, Filiz is a very good artist. All the pictures you see hanging on the wall belong to Filiz. She focused on painting. But she takes part in all positions of our holding. Today she is able to organize a meeting on her own. I appreciate her very much. She is a successful business woman. My son and I are proud of her. She is also the director of the painting course she founded. She arranges and organizes exhibitions.

Her merciful heart, which I love the most and find most admirable, beats with the love of God. Children, don't forget to remember God.

Everything will be fine, don't worry. I hope by the grace of my Lord everything will be alright. Let us remember our Lord in every situation. He's the only one who gives and takes, don't forget that, kids."

How beautifully he spoke, those words were still ringing in my ears. In my hard days I held on to these words, they always gave me strength. These words gave wings even to the wingless, they brought the lost out of the bottomless corner and filled it with hope.

Surround yourself with someone whose
eyes can tell you how much it loves you.
Without having to say a word.

CHAPTER
4

About a week had passed in the meantime.

When they wanted to enroll Suat in a private school, they explained that there was a problem. Because since her mother is still alive, they must have permission from her. They couldn't register him without her permission. In order not to waste any time, they would have tried everything to find my stepmother. So far without success, it was not registered anywhere. It was as if the ground had split open and she was immersed in it. I wish it would be like this!

Was this how a mother oppressed her children? How could she leave her children without thinking? What was that character trait? What was that conscience? Even though she was a mother, how could she leave her children and just go? Well she was gone, but when she leaves, can't a mother hug, kiss and smell her child? Wouldn't she miss your children's scent?

I REJECT (CONDEMN) them…

I REJECT (CONDEMN) those who think as they do...

I DO NOT RESPECT those who leave their children this way...

While Yasemin was recording these words, she had been crying a lot, so many sobs could be heard. Yasemin shed tears for her siblings who were conceived by her biological father and born to the stepmother. Her compassion and conscience were clear because Yasemin raised them. Yasemin took care of her siblings. Yasemin had a heart full of God's love. Yasemin was just a little girl who could not tolerate injustice and ruthlessness. Who had given her siblings the affection and love of their mother and father over the years.

A small heart that had even sacrificed her own life, a person full of wounds and yet full of love.

Yasemin was just one of thousands of Yasemins!

Before Yasemin continued with the recordings, she had recovered quite a bit and was completely normal again. The recording she had interrupted in the morning ended with the continuation in the evening.

When they wanted to enroll me in school, the only problem was not that my parents had died, but that Hikmet and Filiz had no rights over me. They couldn't let me enroll in school without papers.

So Hikmet and Filiz said they wanted to adopt me while we were having dinner after work in the evening. I had received a unique offer from these beautiful people, which once again shocked me positively.

"But how can that be!" I expressed my surprise. Filiz and Hikmet said in their wisdom: "There is no problem, my child. We can't have children. Look at your brother Nihat, he became a teacher because he wanted to and we let him make the decision himself. Nothing happens without a reason, everything is predetermined. Our destiny is predetermined. You saw us, we saw you.

So that you have a good future and we can have children, we have considered adopting you. If you agree, my friend will call the prosecutor and I will forward this petition to him immediately. But since we haven't found your siblings' mother yet, it might be a little problem for them. But it's not a problem for you if you accept that."

How did I know then what adoption was? I had never had anything to do with such things. What can the word adoption mean to someone who has been chasing work, oppressed, despised and undervalued since childhood from dawn to dusk? How could someone who was undervalued know the concept of adoption?

"As you see it," I answered simply.

"IF YOU SEE IT APPROPRIATE."

What a great answer that was, wasn't it?

In the meantime, a large search party had driven to our village and investigated how and in whose car my stepmother had gotten when she left our village. "We'll find her, with God's leave. We have decided to adopt your siblings as well. You have the right to live rightly like any other human being. You also have the right to live your childhood, go to school, dream about your future and have parents," Hikmet said with his compassionate heart.

With my deep wounds burning in my soul, I didn't have the ability to make rational decisions anyway. While they tried to give us the best, I couldn't think of anything to object to.

A few days had passed. Toward evening, when the lord of the household was returning from work, a call came. A person named Ahmet, who had been a shepherd in one of our neighboring villages for years, had seen the car with the two of them. While Ahmet was making his animals drink from the well that was on the side of the road, said car stopped at the well and a man approached it. However, the woman never got out of the car.

"Do you know this person?" He asked the shepherd.

In response to this question, he gave the following information: "He is a car mechanic, he has a car workshop. (He described the location of the workshop). When he gave me his cattle from our neighboring village, I locked them behind a fence of tires so they would not scatter in the areas where I was herder. This person brought me the old tires, but I don't know the man well. There was only one meeting. Why did you ask, brother?"

Hikmet asked politely. "That's enough information. Please tell me Ahmet where you live. Just in case." Then he hung up.

This was an interesting development. We all looked at Hikmet with great curiosity. He was very humble and yet full of hope, he said: "Tomorrow a miracle will happen, we will get closer to the mother of Suat and Kiraz." It may seem unnecessary to some that I just recorded these problems on audio, but it was for me it doesn't. Even just a change of direction, improvement or hint in my life was very important to me. That's why I told everything.

Almost three weeks had passed when Suat said to Filiz for the first time: "Mother!" Filiz sobbed: "My son, my son..." and hugged him. Since then he addressed Filiz as mother and Hikmet as father.

When Kiraz heard that from her brother, she started calling them mommy and daddy, too. So I decided to say Mother Filiz and Father Hikmet.

The day after the phone call, Father Hikmet went to the auto repair shop and confronted the people there about the incident. The man who had taken Suat's and Kiraz's mother away was quickly found. My stepmother asked for an exorbitant amount of money to clear the adoption and Father Hikmet gave it to her. Until now I still don't know how much she asked for.

As Suat and Kiraz's negotiations continued, a private tutor came to our home to tutor them at home. They sent me to a private school. They gave me their last name and adopted me. After school I also started therapeutic treatment with Ms. Nalân. I had kept secrets from many things, I could not express them. Even if I had told it, she wouldn't be able to understand it anyway. Today she was a famous therapist because I often saw her on TV shows where she was invited. She was the daughter of a wealthy family, high society! She was educated, loved and appreciated. If I told her what a village girl like me had gone through, she wouldn't understand. Nalan was warm, yes, she had a sweet, sincere and reliable approach, but I talked about unnecessary troubles because I thought."

She wouldn't understand me." Over time, I only approached her sincerity by answering her questions. When our session was over we would hug and then I would leave.

Mother Filiz always asked me: "Do you understand each other well?"

"Yes," I always said, because I didn't want to upset her.

Sometimes you don't even know what you're going through until you tell someone you love.

Yasemin's Struggle

CHAPTER
5

Months had passed since we were established. The regularity of the daily routine had settled in, we continued our everyday life.

From time to time my brother Nihat also came by. This time it was Mother's Day. Suat and I woke up early. We took out her gift and prepared breakfast. My brother Nihat also came into the kitchen to make preparations. We looked at each other strangely. It was the first Mother's Day and he was stunned to see us preparing breakfast. I quickly apologized to him because he was the older one. "We wanted to surprise our mother Filiz," I explained. "This is great, let's continue the preparations together, as siblings. Let's surprise her together on Mother's Day, " he replies happily. "She actually deserves this happiness every day."

We sat together as a family at the breakfast table and all enjoyed it. In a moment when I was alone with mother Filiz, I asked: "Can I call my aunt who lives in Germany?"

"My child, of course she is your aunt on your mother's side. Protect yourself and your family from people who will hurt you, but of course, if your heart desires it, call them my child. Say hello to her from us, too," she said with a smile.

From the past, I had a little memory box that I called my treasure box, in which I kept all the good and bad things about my past. It also included my aunt's number in Germany. So I picked up the phone and went to my room. I sat down on my bed and opened my treasure chest. A lot of memories flooded my mind at that moment, to be honest I was excited. When I called them, the busy signal came. I waited a while, then called again. This time it rang and my cousin picked up the phone. That's how I introduced myself, but he didn't recognize who I was at first. I think that was completely normal. In a family that lacked communication, not knowing who I was, understandable. Then he gave me his mother on the phone.

"Yasemin? My child, where are you? How are you? Thank God!" She exclaimed, excited and trembling. Her voice surprised me, it reminded me of my mother's voice. "To me, aunt meant being a half-mother, and today is Mother's Day. Aunt, Happy Mother's Day. We're fine, thank God, how are you?" I asked, my voice shaking. "Where are you calling from, my child? Thanks for the call. How are you, are you okay? I died out of curiosity because I didn't know how to reach you and your siblings. you left the village I hear you live in a wealthy family. What you went through, I didn't believe it. I said. My Yasemin isn't like that, or is that true, my child?"

Why did my aunt ask me? "I didn't believe what I heard," she said. But she should have believed it, because that was the truth. Why did she say Yasemin wasn't such a person? "What's it like living in a wealthy family?" She asked.

"What have you heard about me, aunt?" I persisted.

"No, my child, never mind. If it wasn't the truth, you would have said it anyway. I won't tell you and I won't upset you. You're fine, that's what matters. Suddenly you made your voice heard, the world became yours. Thank you, little one, " she said.

"Aunt, what does that mean? I wish I'd called earlier," I said.

Trying to be sincere didn't sound convincing at all. After our phone call, I was lost in thought. I didn't expect a call like that.

I left my room and went to the others. Mother Filiz asked how our phone call went. "She was very curious, her thoughts were probably always with me. She didn't know how and where to reach me. She asked a lot of people to find out where I was, " I replied. Brother Nihat said lovingly, "Yasemin, don't be angry or offended with me. I didn't feel well because you suffered so much from your family and relatives. I don't want you to be upset or hurt. That's why I overheard your conversation on the other phone. I know I violated your privacy, but it was not my intention to abuse it. My goal was to keep you and your siblings away from those who hurt you. So please forgive me, even if it seems rude and disrespectful at first glance. "

In fact, he was right in his own way.

Today was Filizs' mother's day, today was her day. It was a very special day. In fact, every day was like that, but in her words: "I asked my Lord for something, but it didn't happen, the virtue of being a mother. Each time I prayed that my Lord would let me live in His chastity and glory. I wanted a child, He is the supreme Lord, and gave me four. You are my best gifts. You don't have to buy me any presents. I am happy and thank my Lord for making me feel like a mother. "

This woman was a real lady. My mother Filiz was a chaste and dignified woman and beautiful at the same time.

The wounds inside me were deep, like a volcano I lived in. Nobody knew this fire, this pain. I would turn to this subject more clearly and deeply later. At times when my emotions were running too high, I found it impossible to control myself. Sometimes my wounds hurt more. This was the reason I sometimes changed the subject I was talking about.

Every once in a while I just let myself get carried away. We were all on the patio. Suat played ball with Kiraz. Many pictures were taken at that time. We were all very happy. Mother Filiz and I walked among the flowers and roses in the garden. What a deep peace of mind that habit was. Mother Filiz named her flowers with such love and care, which amazed me.

In the evening we went to dinner as a family. It had been a great time. After dinner, mother Filiz prepared the bed for my siblings and read them a book as she did every night. I was in the living room with my brother Nihat. My father, Hikmet, was absorbed in the files in his private office. When mother Filiz came to us, my father Hikmet also joined us. We played with my brother Nihat, mother Filiz and my father Hikmet. During the game, mother Filiz said: "Yasemin, should we invite your aunt, what do you say?" I was very surprised about that. "I don't think we should rush it," I said.

Hope; Sometimes it's a hopeless wait.

Yasemin's Struggle

CHAPTER
6

Almost over a year had passed. My siblings and I were used to our school life. I had even made friends. The friend's value increased even more than it had ever happened before.

Suat took instrument lessons. His main focus was violin, piano and guitar. When they heard that I had talent in my voice, they sent me to vocal training. So I did vocal training outside of school and therapy sessions. We had a good and healthy educational life.

My sister Kiraz had also started school. While everything was going well and orderly, father Hikmet suffered a heart attack. Our family was upset because we were very afraid. He was our father. I remembered very well that I cried a lot like it was yesterday. He was treated in a private clinic for two weeks. My mother Filiz always cried secretly and hid her tears from us. She always stood in front of us with a smile, she never cried. My mother Filiz was like an angel.

When my father Hikmet came out of the hospital, he also called my brother Nihat. "Join us this week, we need to talk face to face as a family," he pleaded. I couldn't sleep through that night because I was curious about what we wanted to talk about. In truth, I was scared and worried.

It was the weekend and my brother Nihat came over, but he was very worried because it was the first time our father had made such a request. The weather was beautiful, we all sat in our large and decorated tent in the garden and watched our father Hikmet as we waited for him to speak. He got straight to the point.

"Listen, this is my second heart attack. Everything proceeds from our Lord. It is not in our nature to resist or object. When our time comes, we will all go to the afterlife. Sooner or later, death will knock on all of us. Don't be afraid of death, don't be afraid to believe in it. My Lord will let us live by faith to our last breath and I hope He accepts our souls as believers. We don't know when a person will go to the afterlife, only God knows. But it's not too late to express my will, thank God. Nihat my son, you are our first sight. You are a good son, God bless you. You have never embarrassed or upset your mother or me over the years. I know you always wanted to be a teacher. Teach and train students. Empty and form. Your mother and I never stood in the way of that. On the contrary, by God's permission we have done everything as you wanted.

My request to you is; go and take over our business, get involved little by little. This holding does not only belong to me, but to all of us. What if, when my lord says your due date is today or tomorrow. Take over my holding and continue the business. My son, do not deprive hundreds of workers of their income, livelihood and bread. If you say my father has a right on me, I want you to fulfill my last will. Come on, get to work as soon as possible, we'll show you everything from start to finish. Your mother and your brother and sisters are entrusted to God first and then to you, my son. I trust you. I am sure you will achieve many achievements. Because you are my children, you know right from wrong. You are the ones who keep the love of God in your hearts. I never doubted you I felt good every time. This is my only will to you."

Nihat's chin trembled. As he listened to our father, he could not control his tears. My mother Filiz held a handkerchief in one hand and father Hikmet's hand in the other hand and wept. We were all stunned after this conversation. Neither of us expected such a conversation, but there were important issues that needed to be discussed.

My brother Nihat said in a trembling voice: "I will not make a mistake, my father. Even if I work the rest of my life, I can't repay you your worth. I promise you; I'll be with you from today I am always with you, but from today I hope that I can accompany you in your business life. I don't want to cause a problem that upsets you, you know that. I will never object to you. Give me a few days, I first have to finish my old working life in order to be able to make a new start with you. "

After this answer, father Hikmet was very happy. He got up and said to my brother Nihat. "Son, you are my first tear," then they hugged and kissed. It was such an emotional moment that we all cried.

My wounds have been anointed. At the time I thought they were cured, but it turned out they were my cure; father Hikmet and mother Filiz.

A few days had passed. My brother Nihat came back and asked my father for a little more time. He mentioned that his stay is longer. At that moment father said, "If the reaper knocks on your door, you will go either prepared or unprepared, there is no time for that. The sooner you come, the better it will be for all of us. This is my last wish to you. Whether or not you sincerely provide yourself is up to you. I made my last wishes to you, my son."

"I'll be here in two days, my father," replied my brother Nihat, keeping his promise. It even took him less than two days. My father felt more comfortable now, this was reflected in all of us. It was a very sensitive time.

My brother Nihat went to holding with my father and mother in the morning. My aunt called from time to time and asked about the situation. The domestics once gave the phone to my mother, Filiz, when I was in vocal training. My mother Filiz said she had invited my aunt and would cover the cost having accepted the offer.

Within a month my aunt and brother-in-law came from Germany for a week. All expenses were covered by my father Hikmet and my mother Filiz. My aunt gave me a big hug the first time we met, I will never forget it. My parents had a very busy time that week and they occasionally had conversations alone. In the meantime I had gotten used to our new life and was afraid of having to make new decisions. I didn't think about going to my aunt in Germany. Especially not at that time when my father had health problems. The truth was, I never wanted to go to Germany. I had become very used to our new family, loved them.

We lived our lives safely, under the wing of those who wanted our welfare. All we had to do was just be genuine and honest people.

Shouldn't it always be like this? Was it hard for a human to be?

Be fair, requires honesty. You'll win both!

Yasemin's Struggle

CHAPTER
7

Months had passed. We all went about our daily lives quite normally. My brother Nihat had also officially started working in the holding company. Everything was shown to him, from beginning to end, with him everything was renewed and changed. He too had started his life from scratch again.

Ramadan was approaching. My father Hikmet said that during the holidays we would go to the summer house together. Everyone was very happy that we went on vacation. It was supposed to be my first vacation, so I was excited.

In one day we would taste three different feelings of happiness, because it was my adoptive parents' wedding anniversary, three days in Ramadan feast and the vacation. We packed our bags and after breakfast we set off. The driver had packed our luggage in both cars. Father Hikmet, my mother Filiz and my brother Nihat were in one car, Suat, Kiraz and I took our places in the other car. We went to Ayvalık for the summer resort. The journey took about five hours. Every now and then my brother Nihat and Suat would make our trip more entertaining with vehicle changes.

Finally we arrived at the summer house, but I couldn't believe my eyes. A three-storey house, a luxurious villa, almost a palace stretched out in front of me. Not even a mansion would compare next to it. There were gardeners, servants, domestic staff, whatever you wanted. A huge terrace, plus a roof terrace with a whirlpool, stretched over the house. The view was great, looking straight down to the sea. Below was the pool, a little further the sea. It was the first time I was confronted with such a sight. I ran excitedly through the house to see all the floors. It was like a dream and today I said it really was a dream. Lived and cherished while I had lived in that time. The view was exceptional and it was my family that made it exceptional. The good days passed quickly. We never wanted to go back, but we had to.

"We'll come back here if you like, you can even come without us. Due to work, we may not always have the opportunity to take a family vacation in the near future. So you can come whenever you want." Father Hikmet offered. So we prepared for our return and after breakfast we set off. This time my brother Nihat went with us, who said: "You have never been alone, you newly in love. At least keep it to yourselves for now."

We sang and had fun along the way. Nihat couldn't get enough of listening to me. We were all in a good mood. After driving for about three hours, we continued driving after a short break. This time our energy was a bit weaker, we were tired.

Suddenly the driver braked abruptly, everyone was shaken.

The noise was still in my ears today. I was confronted with a nightmarish sight that I never wanted to face and thought of. My father's car went off track and got under a truck. The picture was a shock! It was just a single second that changed our lives. My father Hikmet and my mother Filiz died at the scene. Screaming didn't help. They were gone from this world now. Shocked, we ran around the car. Nothing happened to the truck driver, God protected him. But later another car crashed into the back of the truck, seriously injuring the occupants. The road was completely closed, although the ambulance arrived a little late, it was able to pass through these roads and get to the scene of the accident. They got my father and mother out of the car.

People I didn't know held me to keep me from getting close to the accident. My eye saw neither Suat nor my brother Nihat nor Kiraz. I didn't know who was where. I screamed in shock. A helicopter was ordered to take care of the seriously injured. "No no no! It can not be! It does not work! Don't leave us!" screamed Nihat, shocked like everyone else. He knelt on his knees, we were all miserable and broken.

We drove to the hospital together. It was impossible to describe in words the emotions experienced. The wounds were still deep inside me. This picture was still fresh in my memory, I have never been able to forget it since. An indescribable pain, loss of life, a fire, a deep wound reigned in me. The sudden death of my late father Hikmet and my mother Filiz threw me into a deep hole.

My brother Nihat called the house and said a driver should take the children home and take care of them both. So Suat and Kiraz were picked up. There was no more help for my mother and father in the hospital. My brother Nihat and I were both devastated. My face and fingers were numb from crying. I couldn't open them, I was in so much pain it was indescribable. The experience had left deep scars on my soul. It was not possible for me to describe this pain.

My parents' closest friends flocked to the hospital. In good times and bad, everyone was always there. Whether near or far, everyone came. I was too beat to stand up. Everyone came to support me. "You don't die with the dead!" they said to me. Of course we were aware of that. You don't die with the dead, but at least let me experience my pain, right?

They always expected me to be the strong Yasemin and I have always been strong. I had overcome everything; sometimes by getting rid of everything, sometimes by getting deep wounds! From time to time I wondered if such situations were normal. Yes, it seemed possible; I had no one to protect me, to take care of me, except my Lord. But I want to say something else.

Leave me my childhood, this age, my youth. I had failed to be a girl, so how could I feel like a woman today? I had always protected my siblings like a man, I didn't feel like a woman, even though I looked 100 percent feminine! I couldn't even experience femininity because everything I had experienced was a heavy burden on my shoulders.

Actually, I didn't want to jump from topic to topic now, but I was a person who thought out loud. But over the years I had eaten it all up, so in some situations I jumped from topic to topic. Let me stay the way I am. Everyone tried to change me, but I will be me and stay.

Yasemin, who honestly recorded her audio recording for over half an hour crying and sobbing, fell into a deep, black hole. A pain unlike any other pain overcame her.

Yasemin was a strong person! She had a determined, ambitious, hardworking and very patient character. Despite all the pain and deep wounds she had endured, she was still an admirable person, standing firmly on her feet.

If you listened to her audio recordings, you could tell that none of her sentences started with "I". How could it ever begin as I AM? Let's put the word "I" aside, Yasemin couldn't even taste being "YASEMİN". While Yasemin started becoming "YASEMİN", she lost her precious family.

She blossomed with love, opened her eyes with interest, focused on what she saw with value, and as a result, we had a sparkling, pure, very beautiful Yasemin that blossomed.

Let's continue reading what Yasemin will tell us, the fifth cassette and the recording continued as follows:

I was overcome with exhaustion, the world seemed to be collapsing on me. Good people left early. I wandered from room to room in the house, talking to myself and experiencing my grief deep inside me. The house was full, and journalists from almost every TV station came to express their condolences. They were businessmen who were known and recognized throughout the country. Unfortunately, my dear father and mother were no longer with us. Everyone was there except them. I met my brother Nihat at the house. "Yasemin, there are journalists and TV people here, I don't want you to be seen or recognized for your safety. I don't want anything to happen to you. Please stay out of sight until they're gone," he begged me. My brother, who always wanted our welfare and intervened in every negative situation, was right.

If the wreck is returned to its place, a child's heart means that "All the colors of life are faded"!

CHAPTER
8

Germany's cold wind is blowing towards us!

I went upstairs with my siblings and the psychiatrist Ms. Nalân. After Kiraz fell asleep, we had a deep conversation with Ms. Nalân. Maybe she didn't ask consciously, but the question she asked really touched me and made me think. I had never thought about that direction. "Well, what are you going to do now? Where are you going with your siblings? Do you want to live with your relatives who live in Germany? " she asked. Her questions had made me thoughtful and distracted from that day on. Maybe she was right, maybe she was wrong to ask those questions, maybe she wasn't. These questions led me to the idea that I shouldn't forget who I was. I felt a compelling need to reorient my life, albeit unintentionally.

After my brother Nihat reported that the journalists and TV stations were gone, we returned to the crowd. My heart was in pain. But this time I was quiet, quiet and withdrawn. These questions surprised me, it was like: "You don't belong to this family, they took pity on you, the way out is meant for you." That surprised me what had happened. I was sad, very sad...

For the first time in my life I cried for my family who wanted my kindness, who gave me love and most of all hugged me like a real mother and father.

The pain of losing and losing rose and rose within me. Who am I now and where do I belong was the question, I was stunned.

Tomorrow they would be buried. Inside the house, the voices of the Koran grew loud. There were all kinds of people in the crowd; from friendly-looking crocodiles surrounded by falsehood to real tears. I was surrounded by people who had a hard time accepting me and by people who accepted me and then questioned me. I never wanted to be in this situation and I didn't want to stay.

While Suat walked away from this crowd putting his hand on my brother's shoulder, Brother Nihat had tears in his eyes. "Yasemin! he said. We looked at each other in tears, wondering what to say to each other. He hugged us both at the same time. "Don't leave me alone in this crowd," he begged. Nihat was a man with a burning heart, honorable, successful, full of love and compassion. In the last few days I had thought and cried a lot about him.

He stepped protectively between us, put his hands on our shoulders, then walked us back into the crowd. Over time, people scattered, only relatives and closest family friends remained.

The staff relayed an incoming call to my brother. He made a gesture with his hand and asked me to come to him. Putting my head close to him, I whispered. "What happened, who's on the phone?" "Your aunt is at the airport, they saw the accident and the death news on TV. You come here, Yasemin," he answered. Actually, I wasn't happy with this news. Of course, my aunt was not to blame or responsible for any of the incidents I had witnessed at the time. They didn't have to bear the sin of the harm done to me by others. This injustice, this cruelty I experienced was caused by my relatives and family. My confidence was shattered, I was scattered and reactive. I was scared and worried! So I wasn't kind to my family and relatives, but to everyone because they hurt me so much.

From my looks and body language, my brother Nihat understood that I was not happy with this news, that I was scared and worried.

"Have no fear, always keep your heart pure and good, believe in God and in His power. As long as you believe in God with your heart and surrender to Him alone, our Lord will keep evil and evil-minded people away from you and protect you in a circle. As long as you don't lose your faith and love for God, even if the person comes towards you with evil intentions, they cannot enter this circle and harm you. I'll be there too, unless you want me to, then I'll leave you alone with your aunt, trust me!" That was how he reassured me.

About two hours later, my maternal aunt came, and I really knew nothing about her. As soon as she saw me she ran to hug me for all to see.

Everyone ate together, but I wanted to retire to my room because of the rush and fatigue of the day. The staff of the house took care of the guests. So I bade everyone good night after asking permission to retire to my room. As I was walking into our room with Suat, my brother turned to me and asked, "Yasemin! Have you ever thought about why your aunt came and visited you?" At that moment I couldn't answer my brother because I hadn't really thought about it. Occasionally I got questioning looks. I didn't feel comfortable with their observations and the way they analyzed me.

Once I'd retired to my room, Suat started pestering me with questions. But I had suffered so much, both because of my stepmother and because of my biological father. All of my relatives left me alone among people who hurt me. From the violence and unscrupulousness of my stepmother, from the forced marriage, to the slanders and attacks of the villagers, to the rape of my brother-in-law. My family and relatives had not been there for me and had not supported me. Until the hands of my late family reached us, the loneliness of the painful days I lived in, even at this age, left a mark on my face. The question that Suat rightly asked plagued me.

As I lay down on the bed, I thought about and analyzed my brother Nihat's advice. Then I fell asleep without first pulling the covers on.

In the morning I woke up to my aunt's kisses on my cheeks. Suddenly I jumped out of bed, startled. "Don't do that to me again, let me, let me go!" I started screaming and crying. I shivered and slid back against the wall, terrified trying to cover my mouth with my clenched hands. "Get out of my room, get out, get out!" I yelled. My whole body was shaking, it was the first time I experienced such an attack, I was even scared of myself. Because of the nightmares I had been going through, I knelt down, pulled my knees up, clutched them and tried to stop the trembling of my whole body.

While my aunt left the room confused, my brother Nihat entered. Fearful and worried, he ran towards me, took me under his wings and rested my head on his shoulder. "Cry sister, cry! Set your heart at rest. Remember you are not alone, there is God and I am with you. From now on no one will be able to harm you, no one will be able to touch you. Don't be afraid!' he said. I slowly calmed down at his compassionate words. "I was so scared, I was so scared, brother!" I sobbed. When I looked up, I saw my aunt standing in front of the door, her hand over her mouth.

In fact, I was very ashamed of my behavior afterwards. This attack was the result of my fears and nightmares. After I calmed down, I said, "I'm fine, thanks brother. I'll get ready and then come   down."The incident scared me a lot though, I couldn't really recover, but I had a funeral ahead of me. I had to focus my balance on it. Since then I have had these attacks more often.

On the way downstairs I listened in silence to my aunt and brother Nihat talking. In order not to be seen, I hid behind the corridor door in the living room.

While my aunt was asking the why questions, my brother Nihat was nervous and suspicious. So he explained that we were adopted, then she said to my brother: "So Yasemin now has a stake in her fortune?" At this question, he immediately ended the conversation. "I would like to take Yasemin and her siblings with me to Germany. She is not yet 18 years old, after 18 this process can be difficult. Yasemin and her siblings are coming to Germany! I'm her aunt! " She responded with a violent reaction.

Nihat was shocked by this conversation. At that moment, Suat came down the stairs. He came up to me quickly. "Please be quiet!" I asked him.

Then we went down the stairs as normal so as not to get caught. Through the back door we walked through the garden. The family sat at the breakfast table, but my brother Nihat and I had no appetite. "Your aunt wants to tell you something, Yasemin," Nihat said. I looked at my aunt with empty and meaningless eyes.

"Aunt, before we talk, my reaction earlier wasn't about you. I don't want you to be offended by that," I explained. "You will be healed and better," she replied coolly. Not being able to listen to the rest of the conversations, I didn't understand why she was so cold and reactive.

"Sorry Yasemin! I've had bad days too. Since we're all together right now, I want to talk to you about something. You are not yet 18, so I would like you to come to Germany with your siblings. You can't stay here, look, they died. The branch you were holding on to broke. You have no choice and cannot stay here. A different life awaits you in Germany," she said. As she continued her speech, I observed my brother Nihat's reactions. He showed his discomfort speaking by slamming his fork down on his plate. At that moment I too reacted: "Aunt, we have a funeral, please show respect."

"You're right, I apologize to you and to you," she replied with a slight smile. The matter was settled. While the kids and my aunt were having breakfast, our attorney came in with a family friend.

For some reason, at that moment, it always occurred to me that the *profiteers always come first*. There was a reason for that, of course, because they were really out for profit. I could name who was what, what they thought and who they really were. But when it came to implementation, my hands were tied. How could I, who was always supposed to be silent as a child, suddenly open my mouth? But I wasn't afraid to tell my brother Nihat. He himself always put his hand on my shoulder.

We had buried my father and mother. It was very painful, my wound was fresh and bleeding. Only those who have suffered such a loss could understand me. Who else could understand the heart that ached and bled as if its life was lost!

When my mother's close friend, the psychiatrist Nalân, came, she didn't want to leave. I didn't like her behavior lately. It was like she was after my siblings and me. This person who fought for my sake when my late mother Filiz and father Hikmet were alive now came up with new ideas every day to get rid of me.

The greatest battle is in the heart!

CHAPTER
9

A few days had now passed since the funeral. My aunt had left for a few days to sort out her own affairs, to go to her husband's relatives. Ms. Nalân, on the other hand, came and went like she was always making fun of me. "What happens now, where are you going?" she asked. I was starting to feel uncomfortable, but there was nothing I could do. It was like being locked in. Exactly three days after the funeral, when I saw my brother Nihat and Ms. Nalân sitting on the grass in the garden talking, I couldn't help but start listening. She wanted something, I could tell. I understood her intention. My views of her changed from day to day.

I listened from my hiding place for almost an hour and a half. She tried to get into my brother's mind. With his head bowed, he listened with sadness and concern. He answered Nalan by saying two or three words or just shaking his head.

Ms. Nalan had made her intentions clear; she insisted that my siblings and I move in with my aunt. "You are young and good-looking, you have a nice life and a nice career ahead of you. You will become the head of your holding company, your name will be on the list of famous businessmen. You will have a happy home, a warm wife and children of your own. I've said it before. I will say it again today; You will not find a cure for Yasemin and her siblings. If they live here it will be a hindrance to your career and your home," she kept telling him, offering all sorts of methods and options. She said she insists on sending them to Germany. Nihat was stunned. "But that's good! Don't get in the way, they are just kids. Aunt means mother half let her go. Even offer her aunt money. Give her every opportunity. I always want to be by your side. Only with you! " she continued.

It felt like someone was pouring boiling water over my head. "Only with you!" she had said, stroking my brother's face and holding his with the other hand. My brother Nihat must have been influenced by this, because he replies, as if in a trance, "Okay, Nalân, I'll talk to her aunt."

The long-established resident didn't need a guide in his own village, we said, because he already knew his way around there. Now I also understood Ms. Nalân's intention better. Nihat, my brother had been wrapped around her finger. Ms. Nalân, who got my brother's approval, didn't want to waste a minute and started to implement her plans. As she got up, she bent down and kissed my brother Nihat on the cheek. "Everything will be fine, believe me," she said and went home.

At that moment I had decided not to allow my brother Nihat to speak to me. He actually hurt me.

Broken and sad I went to Suat. "Let's go to my room, we have to talk," I asked him. In my room, I looked out the window first. My brother Nihat was in the garden. He wandered around helplessly. In his hand he held a branch that brushed across the grass as if he were in a dreamland.

With my shoulders hunched over, I said to Suat with a sigh, "Come on, my dear, sit on the bed. I have to tell you something." We sat cross-legged across from each other. "Come on, sister, start now," he said, eyes wide.

"My dear, maybe you don't like what I'm about to tell you. But I need to talk to you. In the coming days, new decisions may be made and new directions for our lives may arrive. Maybe we'll have to start over," I said.

"Suat, you got it right. I'm having a hard time explaining it right now. Because I don't know what's up yet, but we will experience innovations. Unfortunately we cannot prevent this. Please look at me my little one. Auntie insisted several times that she wanted to take us to Germany. I also heard her talking to my brother Nihat and I was listening to my brother's conversation with Nalân as well. I have no secrets from you, but we both must have a secret from each other. Ms. Nalân is trying to get into our brother Nihat's mind. "Send them from here to their aunt, " she says. Our brother Nihat is already stricken with what is going on these days. He is sad, lethargic and exhausted. Of course we do too, but Ms. Nalân managed to penetrate our brother's thoughts. Nihat said he would talk to me and my aunt. In other words, he hadn't objected to a single sentence of Ms. Nalan's.

My little one, we have to be ready for new decisions about our future. I'm only fifteen years old, I'm a minor. I don't have the right to decide yet. Maybe if we went somewhere other than my aunt, the three of us would end up in separate orphanages. You would have to separate us. Let's not let that happen Please my dear, let's protect each other. Maybe it'll get worse if we stay here, maybe if we go? I don't know. We started all over again from scratch. Their sudden death shocked us all. But let's not be torn apart. Although what I've heard is bitter, they're actually right. The sad truth hurt my heart. He's our brother, whatever happens, it's okay. Just as long as we stick together."

Curious, Suat asked, "Sister, please don't put me down. Did someone tell you something? What's happening? Why do we have to start over? Tell me, sister, what will you do?"

I had problems and didn't know yet what new situations we would be confronted with.

Suat bowed his head, very surprised by what he heard. He hadn't expected such a decision, so he had to recover mentally first.

I quickly hugged Suat. "You know better, sister, I can't disagree," he whispered softly. "Everything will be fine, believe me," I comforted him. "I wouldn't have made that choice if I was eighteen. The three of us would have rented a house.

So we wouldn't have had to seek refuge with anyone, nobody could then push us around. We'll get used to my aunt over time, and she to us. It's a good thing she came to the funeral, maybe she came from other aspects" Suddenly there was a light knock on the door.

"Yes, come in?" I called. It was our brother Nihat who came in. He was sad, he was stroking Suat's head, he was helpless. "Suat my brother, I need to talk to your sister a bit," he said involuntarily.

Without hesitation, he left the room and closed the door behind him. My brother sat on the edge of the bed and spoke with his head bowed, "I'm very sorry, Yasemin, what's happening to all of us? We buried our mother and father. There are so many developments that I am about to have a mental breakdown. I can't tell what's right and what's wrong. I'm helpless too... I'm sorry and my heart is filled with pain. What to do, how to proceed, I don't know anymore. I am expected to lead the holding company. I don't even know if I'm worthy of my father's throne. Their loss has shaken me deeply. It's like I was buried under the rubble in an earthquake. I feel so helpless and powerless. I'm very desperate, Yasemin, very."

Suddenly Mrs. Nalân entered without knocking on the door. The first sentence she said was, "What the hell, you both got carried away with your conversations." Then she sat down next to my brother Nihat. She stroked his leg with one hand and asked: "Did you tell Yasemin?" He quickly grabbed her hand. "No, be quiet. Please! I haven't told her yet," my brother said desperately.

I couldn't bear it that my brother had or got into any more difficulties.

"Nihat, now if you'll excuse me and you're done, I want to tell you something. I accidentally overheard you talking to my aunt. This problem came up again at the breakfast table. Then I heard that you were talking to Ms. Nalan in the garden. After that I hid there to listen to the rest. It was painful for me to hear that, but it's true. With your permission, I want to decide for myself that we'll go to Germany with her as soon as she comes back," I explained.

I didn't really want to start my speech like that, but to keep my brother from getting into trouble, I didn't put it in a way that would hurt him, but as if I didn't know what I had heard. I certainly didn't want his trust in me to be shaken or diminished.

'I thought it would be better for my siblings and me to go to my aunt's. This is a very serious decision, an important decision that will determine our future. When my aunt comes, I want to speak to her personally. Maybe it's good, maybe bad. I still can't tell the good from the bad. God knows the end,"

I added, then my brother hugged me while weeping. As he hugged me tightly, Nalan's and my eyes met. With a fake smile, she replied, "Someone will be very happy with our departure."

My brother wasn't himself, he was exhausted and tired. This is what Ms. Nalan wanted. I didn't want to disturb or burden anyone with our presence. When a person has no mother or father, even where his home was, he feels like a foreign body. Every spoken word pierced my heart like a needle, it hurts. This was one of the disadvantages of being an orphan.

Ms. Nalân had planned it well, because the same day my aunt came back from her husband's relatives. "My aunt is coming today, I'll talk to her myself," I insisted.

As the two were about to leave the room, Ms. Nalân said to my brother with all her impudence: "Look, I told you. Luckily she's leaving now. What would have happened if she only left in the future after she exploited you? She'd stab you in the back with a dagger, that's for sure." She was getting worse every day. I didn't say anything to that, I couldn't either, out of shock.

After being alone in my room, I immediately got out of bed and got my albums out of my drawer. In this house I had learned to learn and live in order to be happy. Today I was just sad. I only felt warmth for my late mother Filiz and my late father Hikmet. May you rest in peace, may my lord bless you abundantly.

I couldn't get enough of their love. They gave me and my siblings so much love. Wistfully looking at their pictures, I cried and stroked their faces with my hands, then I laid them on my heart caringly and crying. My decision was now complete. Actually, I wanted to resist not going to my aunt's, but there was nothing I could do. After hearing the conversations, I couldn't stay here any longer. What beautiful pictures we took together. How we all laughed at the pictures. There, in this house, I had spent the happiest time of my life with my family. It was the first time I had laughed and beamed like that. For the first time I looked at my future with hope. Their love, growing day by day, was balm for my wounds.

But with their loss it was all over. My hopes, dreams and goals faded before my eyes.

I dived into the past and let myself go. There was a knock at the door. My aunt silently entered, but I wasn't ready to speak yet. 'I'm coming now, aunt. Go downstairs,' I said.

"Okay, hurry up, I have something to tell you," she replied.

So I just put the pictures down, then followed my aunt downstairs. Ms. Nalan and my aunt had already become close friends. Of course they would get along well because she sent the money to my aunt. Even if it was difficult for me, I tried not to let these attitudes and this side of me show up. Now I understood my aunt's intention, which snapped me out of my thoughts. "Let's go talk in the garden," she asked me.

Soon I would be a passenger going to Germany!

While she looked around to see if anyone was there, I took the floor: "Aunt, we've decided we'll come to Germany with you." However, I didn't feel any joy from her, and it was she who put this idea into everyone's heads implanted. She had always said: " Luck is on my side, I wish myself the best of luck. " I didn't understand this statement, what she meant. Suddenly I was very scared of my aunt when she said: "When you are eighteen they will pay you your share. If what I'm saying bothers you, you don't have to listen to me." "Aunt, do you hear what you're saying?" I asked. It didn't go in my mind how anyone could think like that. So I wondered if I needed to relive the painful days of the past.

My aunt rushed in and retreated to the kitchen to talk to my brother Nihat. Since it was about us, I followed them without hesitation. My aunt presented him with a fait accompli. 'You give me all the children's papers, at least a copy for now. This information is necessary for the entry application so that I can take it with me to Germany. I have to make an inquiry as soon as possible so that they can come as soon as possible,' she said impertinently. "Okay, but all the documents you need are with our attorney. I'll ask him to send it to you,' he replied.

"No, I won't go without one," she insisted. "Well, let me call him to bring them all," my brother said. The next day my aunt would fly back to Germany. When many people came and went, time passed very quickly. For a moment I caught Nihat alone. I wanted to talk to him, but suddenly Ms. Nalan was there again, she never left my brother alone. In the morning, even before we woke up, she came to us and left late in the evening. With her demeanor and actions, she was no longer old Ms. Nalan. She had gone through a major change, she had succumbed to her ego. So I started to be the old unhappy Yasemin again. The world is collapsed for me.

They say that man gets used to everything, not so.
You put up with it because you don't really
have a choice, but you can't get used to it...

CHAPTER
10

It had been almost a month when my brother and I could only speak two or three times. Due to his constant phone calls, we could never end our conversation. He worked a lot, he was rarely at home during the day. We also went to school, but my brother was withdrawn from music education and it was decided that I no longer needed a psychiatrist either. The meetings were suspended. When Ms. Nalân came to us, I had been helping the staff with the housework.

In the meantime, my aunt called my brother and told us that our application to enter Germany had been approved. Passport and visa matters have been initiated. Of course, it was the lawyer Mustafa and Ms. Nalân who did it. Somehow I had the feeling that something was between the two. When they were with us and felt unobserved, they would whisper and laugh together in the corner by the shore. My brother still didn't know what was going on.

Ms. Nalân was eight years older than my brother, she wrapped him around her finger. She had seduced my brother with her flirty approaches. Nihat was pure, benevolent, pure-hearted, dependable, and knew right from wrong. He was a compassionate and conscientious person. It was incredibly painful for me to see how the warm family atmosphere was destroyed day by day. My late mother and father didn't deserve that.

At a moment when I happened to meet my brother alone, I said: "We have to have the Koran read, my mother and father have been dead for almost forty days." Immediately Ms. Nalân was there again, entering the room. She had a file in her hand, she was busy with her organizational work, she was constantly on the phone and talking about orders and agreements. My conversation with my brother was interrupted. However, she was the one who was disrespectful and interrupted us because she was on the phone right here next to us so as not to leave us alone. My optimism towards her had been completely lost. My confidence was shaken and I was disappointed. Something was organized, but I didn't quite understand what.

I looked at my brother questioningly, then asked them out loud, "What's going on?" My brother closed his eyes, nodded with a slight smile, then ignored his next calls. "Brother, I said our parents are approaching their fortieth day. We should have the Koran read,' I repeated. Ms. Nalân, who cut off her phone as soon as she took off her headphones, scolded me greatly! I was surprised. 'Undisciplined, immoral... Poor and uncivilized creature. Don't you see I'm on the phone, you're talking, get out of here. My wedding preparations are interrupted because of you, get out, go to your room immediately!" she barked at me.

Stunned, I stared at my brother, just before I left the room, he grabbed my arm. "Yasemin, this is Nalan's excitement. She's busy organizing, she's a little stressed," he said defensively.

Suddenly I didn't know my brother anymore... God only knows how I came into my room with shaking knees and how I cried after throwing myself on the bed. My brother wanted to marry this Nalan! I prayed for my aunt to complete the process as soon as possible. Who previously didn't want to leave this house now prayed that it would be over as soon as possible.

Voices came from the garden, so I went to the window. A man was walking through the garden with Ms. Nalân and my brother. Together they continued their organizational work. Something needs to be built here and there. Files lay in his hands, calls kept coming in, and new people rushed in to prepare for the wedding. Now it was clear what was going on. However, my brother was too blind to see the truth, he was crazy. It was as if these Nalân and their lawyers had been waiting for this one opportunity for years. My poor brother was also a victim caught in their trap.

I wanted to capture a quiet moment and talk to him as soon as possible. I felt compelled to do this. If there was any chance of getting away from Ms. Nalân, I had to talk to him. I had to talk to him in the next day or two at the latest. We were all lost.

As the negativity built up with extraordinary speed day by day, there was a knock on the door of my room and my brother came to me. Being so distracted, I didn't even notice that he had left the garden.

Immediately he started talking: "Come on, my emotional little sister." He lovingly wrapped his arms around me and kissed my forehead. Now was the moment to speak to him, so I jumped at the chance: "Brother, we need to talk, it's very urgent, very important. Please let's go outside, we can't be open with each other here. I have very urgent and very private matters to discuss with you, please don't put it off until tomorrow. Tomorrow may be too late for everyone. "

"Okay, Yasemin, let me finish my work, then we'll definitely have this conversation," he offered.

"No, by then it will be too late. We have to talk today, tomorrow at the latest. Please, until now I have not insisted on anything, I have not asked anything of you. Please! This conversation is very important, we have to talk!" I insisted, when suddenly Ms. Nalân appeared, who had overheard everything.

"What did you want to talk about, what is so urgent, what is so special? Or are you secretly talking behind me?' she hissed at me. My brother immediately intervened: "No, please Nalân, do not create anything that does not exist. Yasemin wanted to talk, I think because of her aunt. Tomorrow Yasemin and I will go out alone for a while, drink our tea and talk, don't tease your sweet soul," he said, squeezing my chin and smiling into my face. Ms. Nalân took my brother's arm and led him out of the room. He looked warmly into my eyes, then closed the door. She poisoned my last days with her attitude. I was afraid of harming my brother so when we met I had to be very sensitive with him to warn him because he was unaware of what was happening, what changes were taking place. Whenever I got the chance, I wanted to show him that Ms. Nalân only had her own interests in mind. But I had no evidence, how should I put it, that it didn't upset or hurt my brother.

If my late mother Filiz and my father Hikmet were alive, they would not have allowed this and set their limits. Because they were good people and could tell good from bad.

After staying in my room for a while, I went downstairs. I continued to play the three monkeys, hear no, see no, speak no, against Ms. Nalan. "Dinner is ready, come to the table," we were called. My brother and I sat in our usual place. This time there were several extra plates on the table. The others were in the garden, the voices of the crowd getting closer. Apparently a couple of guests were present. With champagne and wine glasses in her hands, she approached the table. We also stood up respectfully, but the stern look from Ms. Nalân met us, who said very harshly: "You eat inside", while pointing to the staff kitchen. His, or rather her, guests were still laughing. My brother got up immediately, held my shoulder and pushed me towards the kitchen.

"There are adults and there are magazine journalists, so maybe that's why she said that. Did she hurt you, my dear?" he asked me.

This time I couldn't hide my reaction, so I huffed, "What's the matter with you? And who are the minors with your guests? Have fun!" So I just went into the kitchen and left him there. It became more unbearable every day. There were many things that went unfair, but I had to get through those few days. My brother didn't usually drink, but he started drinking.

A lot went wrong. We were confronted with attitudes that should not have happened. In the kitchen, the gardener's wife, our aunt Meral, who of course wasn't my biological relative but was part of the household staff, took care of Kiraz's food. My aunt Meral, was a kind hearted woman, she had always taken care of Kiraz. I thanked her sincerely for that. To this day, on holidays and special days, I still call her and ask how she is. She was human like an angel.

After dinner we retired. I used the house phone to call my maternal aunt. However, she was on the phone to someone, so I gave up and said to myself, "No, no, tomorrow." So I left the phone and went upstairs to my room. Fighting the tide with mixed feelings, I was really just trying to get through everything. Day by day, the silent cries of despair grew louder within me. This feeling made my heart pound, it was like suffocating.

That evening I was so bored that I lay on my bed and got deep in thought. In my own way, I fought my feelings by shaking myself.

My late father Hikmet had given me a book even though it wasn't a special day like my birthday or something. Just because I like reading books. I read without breathing. I got up in desperation and took the book off the shelf. For two days, as soon as I got home from school, I read it to page one hundred and seventy-four. Right now I was engrossed in the cover photo. I really liked the content of the book. All the injustices that an unfortunate girl went through made me sad, but I could have been that person because I recognized myself in this book. From that day to this day I follow the author of this book.

My room didn't have a balcony so I went to my brother Suat's room who was lying on his bed watching TV. He immediately got up and greeted me as if I were a visitor. This warm approach was very good. "I want to read on your balcony," I said to him. So we spread a blanket on the balcony, pushed out the table, and took a glass of lemonade with us. It was very tiring, but I wanted it that way.

With my face down on the cover and my hand on the page, I began to read again. The atmosphere that evening was really relaxing! The only sound I heard was the clicking of cats paws and the barking of dogs that the book conveyed to me. Like I'm in the story.

Suddenly I heard a noise from below, which distracted me. The door of the terrace was open, I could tell from the sound of heels that it was Ms. Nalân, who was walking around and talking to someone on the phone very quietly, almost in a whisper. It was weird for me. Actually, it shouldn't have bothered me at all because it was Ms. Nalân. But you should always be ready for anything. Since she was whispering, her conversation was difficult to understand. This time I turned my attention to her. Even though I knew they weren't listening, I listened anyway because I was very suspicious of her.

I couldn't believe what I heard. This Ms. Nalân spoke secretly to our family lawyer, Mustafa. I had sensed before that there was something between them and believed they had a secret relationship. When I heard what they were talking about,

I figured I shouldn't feel guilty that I hadn't violated their rights because I didn't take their sin upon myself. But there were other things that bothered me about their conversation. Of course I was surprised when I heard that they cheated on my brother Nihat. A trap was set for him, they had given my aunt a large amount of money to take us and she would even get another payment.

"Most of it is gone, little is left, be patient, my dear," she said. "We are getting closer to our goal every day."

My aunt from Germany had received her payment of one hundred and fifty-thousand lira as an investment through fraud. I was surprised at that. How did my brother become so blind that he didn't see it? I had thought a lot about why he wasn't seeing things. A day later, they would pay my aunt another hundred thousand lira. This woman did her best to get us out of here. Hopefully my brother would wake up quickly and understand who these people were. "My dear, there are voices from inside, don't bust me. I'll be with you by seven tomorrow morning at the latest," she ended the call. What kind of a snake is this!

My enthusiasm for reading was still alive, but it was late. So I cleaned up Suat's balcony, took the blanket and put the table and the lamp back inside. Before leaving the room, I tucked my brother in and kissed his forehead.

My head was tingling, I wasn't tired yet. Under the covers, I thought about what to talk to my brother about. Above all, I had to say exactly what I wanted to say without upsetting or offending him. Since I didn't talk to him about such things, I couldn't predict his attitude and reaction. Eventually I fell asleep thinking about it. The next morning I frantically looked for my aunt Meral all over the house. However, I couldn't find them. Through the window I saw the gardener Uncle Osman, so I went out to ask him where she was. That's how I found out that my aunt Meral was taking care of the new household staff.

Anyway, I thought she was busy at the moment, so I went back to my room and planned to talk to her later when I got back from school. After I got dressed, I went into the kitchen with my school bag.

Kiraz sat on my aunt Meral's lap, who showed the new employees where the supplies were. Our breakfast table was also ready.

"If you want to leave Kiraz with me, Aunt Meral, you can relax and get on with your work," I offered. "My arm is already breaking off, my girl, that would be great," she answered me in her own words. I quickly approached the table and sat Kiraz on the child's chair. "You better feed her. Come on Suat, I have to show our new staff around the house, " she said.

Before she left I added, 'We need to talk urgently after school today, Aunt Meral. Things happen in this house that you can't even imagine. I should definitely tell you that." Suddenly Ms. Nalân was standing right behind me at the entrance of the kitchen, listening to what we were talking about. Suddenly she rudely interrupted my words: "Let's hear what's strange going on in this house? Tell me so we all know." She gave me a sly smile.

"Yasemin dreamed, she told me her dream," my aunt Meral replied. Her name should have been Melek (Angel), not Meral. My angel aunt. How could she cover up the subject immediately. Without looking at Aunt Meral's face, Ms. Nalân said, "Are these my new employees here?" My Aunt Meral, very embarrassed, said, "Yes, they arrived last night, Ms. Nalân. I showed them around the house and showed them their tasks and business areas," she replied.

"Then why are you standing here useless, go about your work!" she was harsh on my aunt Meral, who left the kitchen without answering. I became angry at this woman's attitude. How could she see herself in the upper class and use her eyes and words to talk down and insult Aunt Meral like that? But I couldn't do anything because I was also one of their victims at the time. She had silenced us so much that we all felt like victims. Not wanting to be in the same room with her,

I got Kiraz off her chair, took her breakfast and left the kitchen. While I was going to my room, Suat came down. "Don't go down, don't let your mood spoil too. I'll get us toast from the buffet," I said.

Because I had to go to school, I left Kiraz to my aunt Meral again. How much could I have helped my aunt even if I had been at home?

Weeks had passed since my maternal aunt had flown to Germany. The time went by so fast, it felt like just yesterday. After school we had lunch with Suat. I was afraid to leave without warning my brother and without providing important evidence. In a way, I wanted to protect him.

The day finally came when I got the chance to talk to him. There were only two newly arrived employees in the house, Aunt Meral, Uncle Osman, Kiraz, Suat, the driver and myself. For the first time I felt good again.

Curious, I asked Uncle Osman: "Why did our people leave, why did new employees come?" "My daughter, eat your grapes, don't ask about the vineyard. If we don't know, that's for the best. Don't concern yourself with these problems," he replied. Then the driver and my uncle Osman went out too, so we were alone in the kitchen with my siblings and aunt Meral.

To reiterate, even this kitchen resembled that of a luxury restaurant. All domestic workers met there to prepare the meals and all organizational work was done from there. The actual kitchen was in another room. The kitchen cabinets were made of acrylic in a brilliant white. There was an exit door to the front terrace like in a palace. As we walked from the kitchen to the dining room, we were greeted by a dining table that seats twelve. Everything was very luxurious.

Anyway, I didn't want to get off topic. As I was speaking, I suddenly remembered my aunt Meral telling me something. "The question you just asked your uncle Osman was thoughtless. Be very careful who and where you ask, my daughter. Ms. Nalân dismissed the old staff, instead she took these two in their place. You must be careful, my daughter, with these two collaborators chosen by Ms. Nalân. I've noticed both of them. Oh! Oh! Ever since the householder Filiz and the householder Hikmet died, this house is not the same as before. We gotta keep our eyes open, my girl. This woman will soon be showing us the door too" she rightly warned me at the time with caution!

She must have felt something too. Maybe she overheard a few conversations like I did. Maybe she was playing the three monkeys like me, but she knew something. Otherwise she wouldn't talk like that, she wouldn't want to advise and warn me like a mother.

"Aunt Meral, I wanted to talk to you about these things too, if it was convenient for you. Ms. Nalân is playing a tricky and very bad game with my brother Nihat. We must warn my brother, he is in danger. He's being set in a big trap, I heard what was said with my own ears," I told Aunt Meral, who immediately tried to silence me.

"Don't talk about such things at home, Ms. Nalân comes from every corner. She's just everywhere, you know that. Let's go to the garden," she suggested in haste and concern. Now I could finally explain what I had seen, because it still took a while for my brother to come back home. Ms. Nalan rarely came to see us when my brother was away.

We were sitting at the table when she said, "Come on, tell me what you heard, my child." So, from start to finish, I told her everything I knew and had heard.

It was certainly she who had planned our departure to Germany, who gave my aunt a large sum of money, because a large amount was again paid from the holding account, from the accounting, which was written off as holding investments and therefore did not go unnoticed would. I told her that she had a secret relationship with our lawyer, that she only got in touch with my brother Nihat because of his wealth, even that the wedding was planned. "My brother is about to fall victim to a wicked trap. We must warn him, Aunt Meral.

When the deceased master and lady of the house were still alive, this woman did not show her true colors. Now her true colors and intentions are clear," I said, speaking what I was thinking. We dealt with each topic individually and talked about it in detail.

What could she actually do, she was also a kind of victim. When Ms. Nalân hurt her in the kitchen, she didn't even answer. "Nihat is considered my son, he grew up in my hands, I raised him. Nihat was to me what your sister Kiraz is to me now. He has changed a lot lately, mostly due to the influence of Ms. Nalân. He actually knows something is wrong, but he still grieves because the home side died. My son knows right from wrong, but in fact these sudden deaths have left us all confused, shaken, and left under the rubble like an earthquake, so it will take time to recover, to pick himself up," explained Aunt Meral.

She too was in pain. Yes, she was right. Although we had only lived in this house for two and a half to three years, we were shaken. I loved family more than my own mother and father. I don't want to be unfair to my late mother, but I was only seven years old when she passed away. My mother loved me very much. Most of the memories of her were, of course, forgotten from my memory due to my age.

But while we were trying to draw together, Ms. Nalân did what she could to tear us apart. "I need to speak to my brother as soon as possible, without further obstacles. Please help me, Aunt Meral," I begged her. "My child, I will do what I can, but you must protect yourself from Ms. Nalân's evil tricks. She tempted my son. You are right, we must protect ourselves, but we must not fall victim to their evil and devious traps. We should always be on the side of good, my child," she said kindly. It was okay, it was enough for me that she said it. The most important thing was being able to explain what was going on. Not only I, but actually everyone at home had noticed the change, but because they were afraid of Ms. Nalân, nobody commented on it.

She then confessed to me her doubts about the new housekeeping staff. Several times that day she told me that I had to be very careful with them. A scam was afoot, but sooner or later the scams would be exposed. Everything she said confirmed my concerns. While I was listening to my Aunt Meral, there were some in my late parents' bedroom. The curtains played and wobbled back and forth. As I continued to listen to Aunt Meral, the curtains in my room shook as well.

Gradually enough! It was enough!

On those days only my aunt Meral had entered the masters' bedroom. Besides that, my brother had come in two or three times, but no one else. Still, the curtain shook again, who was in the bedroom?

I quickly interrupted my Aunt Meral, "Aunt, our new staff is at work. I saw the curtain swing twice," I said, pointing from the garden towards the window. "My child, don't be fooled, don't look.

We're going in now," she replied. That's exactly what we had done, suddenly we heard quick footsteps from above, heading for the stairs. They must have seen us because they left the room to avoid being caught by us.

What were they doing in the bedrooms? I always thought of that.

My brother Nihat should have awakened immediately from that unconsciousness, that deep sleep that was paralyzing him. Whatever happened, I was determined to tell him the truth. While there was still time and before I went to Germany, he had to find out everything. Our passports were already ready, we were just waiting for our visa. I was told it should be delivered tomorrow.

Aunt Meral's husband, whom we always called Uncle Osman, wanted to buy suitcases. "My child, buy the suitcases with Uncle Osman alone today. I have work to do here," Aunt Meral asked me. *Her commitment must have been to train two new employees* because she hadn't told me.

My Aunt Meral was right again, the visas would be ready soon. It was necessary to prepare the suitcases. Thirty kilos per person were allowed, that's what I was told at customs. *How am I supposed to fit my whole room into those thirty kilos?* It was impossible. I had only the best memories of this place. What came to my mind were the pictures rather than the things I wanted to take with me, just to remind me of that good time. The last remnants of that time.

My aunt Meral is an old woman, she would definitely interrogate the newly arrived staff secretly when we went to pick up our luggage. We got ready with Suat and went shopping with my uncle Osman.

A few hundred meters from the house was the inconspicuous wooden restaurant with a small entrance. From the outside it looked too old to want to go inside. It had a warm atmosphere with a view of the city from above, but once inside it was too warm to want to leave. In addition, it was a place by the stream and in contact with nature. It was a cute place with a capacity of about fifty guests, plus there were tables outside. Suddenly I noticed the lawyer's car in front of this restaurant.

What was he doing here, he didn't live nearby? I immediately informed my uncle Osman that I had seen the lawyer's car. "My daughter, he must be eating, let him eat. You just ignore it." he answered.

So I followed the advice he gave me. A little further in the parking lot of the shopping center overlooking the roadside, Ms. Nalân's car was also parked.

"Oh, Uncle Osman! There is no such coincidence. Look, here is Ms. Nalan's car! They're messing up our lives, they're plotting something. "Don't say that, don't talk like that," he admonished me.

My driver Ahmet laughed at that moment because my sentence came across as sarcastic. My uncle Osman said, "My child, didn't I tell you not to see what you see." When we got back in the car, I sighed deeply because nobody wanted to intervene. However, if we had entered this restaurant, we might have seen them at a table and heard what they are planning for a new trap, who knows. It was they themselves who allowed such thoughts. Why didn't I have such thoughts about kind-hearted, well-meaning people? I sat in the car like a naughty little girl. However, in my own defence, I wasn't a naughty girl or a spoiled girl at all, or circumstances didn't allow for it.

After we bought our bags and returned home, Ms. Nalân and the family lawyer encouraged us to go to Germany. "What coincidence?" I said, thinking out loud. Uncle Osman admonished me again:

"My child, please shut up. You could be heard," he nudged my arm lightly. Actually he was right, because I should have kept quiet until I had spoken to my brother. While my Aunt Meral prepared the meal with one of the newly arrived employees, the others set the table for dinner. Apparently guests would come, a very pompous table was prepared. Thinking we couldn't talk to my brother anymore, I retired to my room.

Life is a circle!

CHAPTER
11

Three days had passed.

I said to my brother Suat, "Now we have to pack our things. Just put everything that's important to you that you don't want to leave here in one place in your room." He said he'd already started. I was the one who didn't start packing since I was playing detective. While everyone was ready to go, I was busy getting ready. If my brother didn't have time to talk, I would leave that task to Aunt Meral. Time passed pretty quickly.

A miracle could change everything. My excitement increased. I wanted it all to be over as soon as possible. In my room I put the things that were most important to me together. My brother had offered me a few days ago: "Every time you come, you can take something with you, or if you want, I'll send you everything by ship or plane, whatever you want."

Aunt Meral agreed: "He'll just ship it to you by ship. Listen to your brother!" Of course I agreed. Since my brother was going through a very busy time, I didn't want to tire him out with these issues and my special requests. So I said hesitantly, "No! No! Let's not bother!" But it won't be a change of location, nor will it be a stone's throw from Germany. That was of course the most logical decision.

In the end, my siblings and I packed our personal belongings into a large container and had them shipped. However, it was unclear when it would arrive in Germany. It didn't matter anyway. Thanks to my Aunt Meral and Uncle Osman, who arranged everything so that we could ship our things by container, we would have everything with us. Even if we took everything with us, we still left very special memories in this house that would never be forgotten.

One thing caught my attention again, Ms. Nalân kept whispering to the lawyer. My brother Nihat would be coming home soon. Maybe he wanted to tell me let's talk today, maybe one day he definitely would. Various dishes were quickly prepared in the kitchen should guests come. She wanted us to leave before the wedding, I heard that from Ms. Nalân that day when she spoke to this lawyer. The lawyer also used the holding company's money to decide which transactions were to be made. That way they got rid of us faster.

Coyotes! Their deceptions would be exposed sooner or later. *But I had always wished it would come out before it was too late.* Ms. Nalân behaved as if she were the mistress of the house.

The dining table was well appointed with a luxurious table setting. The expected guests came one after the other. We were asked to get out of the way. We didn't want to be there anyway.

Well, I said to myself: *"Yasemin, listen to your uncle Osman, don't make your aunt Meral sad, be patient. You're going anyway."* For the past few days, I'd wished I could avoid breathing in the same environment with her, so the time would pass more quickly.

My brother Nihat wasn't back yet. After we had eaten we retired to our room. We had settled into our suitcases and packed the things that Aunt Meral had washed and ironed for us.

Suddenly, Aunt Meral hurriedly entered the room, then immediately closed the door. "My child, I heard the lawyer calling. He spoke to a gentleman from the consulate who prepared your visa. During the conversation I overheard him saying that he would transfer the money straight away and thanked him for his hard and fast work. My child, you have to be afraid of them. These people have their hands everywhere. How did they complete these transactions in a matter of weeks, but only with bribes. He then immediately called your aunt and told her he would book a plane ticket for her and give her 100,000 liras if she came direct. My child, you were right. I also heard that they give your aunt money to get you out of here. I don't know the exact day when she will come. Maybe today, tomorrow, or in the next few days, my child. What kind of aunt is she who charges a lot of money to take her nephews and nieces?

My God, protect my three humble children from trouble. Don't abandon the oppressors. Make them strong, equip them and surround them with your patience and strength. Oh, my child, oh woe! If your aunt has accepted the money, I don't want to think about the future any further. Oh woe! No, no, I have no more words to say. Protect yourself always, my child, your brother and sister are trusted to you by God. Always stand up for them, do not remain silent about cruelties, do not play the three monkeys. Yasemin, always fight my child okay? In every situation, God is always with you, my child," she said, then hugged me, crying.

It was like she knew what was going to happen to us. She was now aware of what was going on. Now there was someone who confirmed what I had heard and seen. That's why I felt a relief. Even if I left here, we had our Aunt Meral, our guardian angel, who could testify to everything.

Aunt Meral had gone back downstairs so as not to attract attention. It struck me as strange that we acted like we didn't know anything. My brother Nihat came late. He worked hard. Almost four hours had passed. From time to time I had taken the elevator to the kitchen. Then I got the news from my aunt Meral or my uncle Osman that my brother was still working.

"Go to school tomorrow, Yasemin, these are maybe your last days. We do not know it. Say goodbye to your friends," my uncle Osman advised us.

Yes, it was time to say goodbye. I didn't like goodbye moments. It stank of separation. "Okay," I said, wishing them both a good night and retiring to my room.

Of course I couldn't fall asleep right away, my head was tingling again.

Even though I went to bed late at night, I woke up on time for school time. After washing my hands and face and getting dressed, I went downstairs to the kitchen. Like every morning, Uncle Osman was busy in the garden. Aunt Meral, on the other hand, prepared our breakfast in the kitchen, who spoke to the other new employees in a slightly strained dialogue.

"Aunt Meral, what's the matter?" I asked before I could say good morning. "It's okay, my child, come have breakfast first," she replied. Something didn't go well. Experiencing the same things day after day had become really unbearable. One of the new hires said snotty to my Aunt Meral, "Oh, you're washing my head, shut up, get to work!"

I stood up abruptly. "Say, you're going to apologize to Aunt Meral right away!" I snapped. At that moment my brother Nihat walked in. Finding this to be an awkward conversation, he inquired, "What is going on?". Aunt Meral again with that motherly spirit, "Nothing my son, come. Come on, you eat your breakfast, I made it inside," said to Suat. But I couldn't take it anymore and told how the new staff treated my Aunt Meral.

Then Nihat raised his eyebrows. "Look, whatever Aunt Meral tells you in this house, that's how it's done. I don't want to hear any objections. Don't bring new habits to the old village. And tries to get along well with each other. Aunt Meral is in charge here," he said, slightly sleepy. Suddenly one of the two contradicted: "But Ms. Nalân doesn't say it like that."

"I'm in charge of this house, Ms. Nalân has no authority here," my brother said.

It was the first time that such an unpleasant situation arose in this house, otherwise there was always a warm family atmosphere with the employees. Troubled days began in this house. No one had previously refused their respect. No one had raised their voice in years.

Perhaps my brother was not aware that it was this Nalan who was looking after the house at the time. But hey, I was very pleased and happy that he had approached her like that. "Come to breakfast, Yasemin," he asked me. When I replied, "I have breakfast here," he was surprised and asked, "Why?" "Ms. Nalân wants us to eat here," I explained. "What did you say?" he asked, frowning and getting angry.

"Brother, don't be angry, we're going today or tomorrow. The most important thing is that you are happy." I replied.

He shook his head in surprise. "So we have more to talk about," he said. Aunt Meral took my plate from the table and we left the room. Significantly, Aunt Meral made an eyebrow-eye sign to mean, "Let's see, it's good, take this opportunity to speak." I nodded and winked at her as I followed my brother into the dining room. I had a very positive memory of those days that unfolded at an unexpected moment.

"Come on, let me know what you have to say, don't keep your brother waiting any longer. What do you want to talk to me about urgently?" he asked me to talk. Maybe the breakfast table wasn't the right place to bring up the subject. Because this wasn't a five minute topic to talk about. "Not here, brother, we must speak in a comfortable and quiet environment. I don't want to talk about these issues in the house." I explained. "Okay, let's go out tonight, what do you say to that? Just the two of us, we can talk comfortably. If you like, we can also inform Nalân and Suat," he offered.

There was nothing I hadn't tried to facilitate this conversation. Of course I had done everything possible, now I was deeply depressed. "Brother please, this conversation is very important to me. It should only be between the two of us. Neither Ms. Nalân nor Suat should come with you. Listen,

I'm leaving today or tomorrow, who knows when we'll get that opportunity again. " I said.

"You still have a few weeks ahead of you, wait, but you're in a hurry. Okay, we'll talk among ourselves and in private. We'll both go out after I'm off," he promised. The first sentence he uttered was proof of how ignorant he was. He didn't even know that our visa was issued, that my aunt was coming to get us today or tomorrow. After Nihat had breakfast, he got up quickly. He mentioned that he had important appointments.

"Let me clean up today." Aunt Meral offered. "Come on, get yourself and Suat ready. Let your uncle Osman take you to school, say goodbye to your friends and teachers. In the meantime, I'll prepare something nice for you on the way to Germany," she said warmly.

"Would you like to go?" No one asked me. Yes, nobody had ever asked me if I wanted that. Well, I had kept silent because this was my destiny. I had accepted everything in silence.

After getting ready and saying goodbye to school, we headed back home. There was news that Aunt Meral told me: "Your aunt is getting on the plane at six o'clock." Ms. Nalân was at home, I heard that from her speech. "You will speak to your brother tonight, my child. You won't have another chance," she added.

She was right, I really should talk to my brother tonight. I was in a hurry to retire to my room and finish packing my suitcase. There was almost nothing left in my room. We had already sent everything by container. The most precious thing for me was still with me. I was really very sad because I didn't want to leave. We had entered a new life, we had created an immaculate order for ourselves. But it was one of the facts of life that we had to go. I hadn't had lunch that day because my brother had said, "We're going to a restaurant for dinner alone, we eat and talk."

After I finished packing my personal belongings, I helped Suat, telling him, "We should always be together. We should never be separated from each other. You should always trust me I'm your older sister and Kiraz is our mutual sister. Whatever happens, always trust me, never lose your trust. Unity is strength. We don't know what will happen in Germany. Together we are strong, my dear brother. " With these words he too found some strength.

However, I was afraid, but I could not express it. Maybe I wouldn't have been so scared if I hadn't heard about the money. There was no healing for the dead and the lying, and I sought my peace among the negativities.

Suddenly Aunt Meral came hurrying over to us. "Your aunt is here, my daughter. The driver will bring them here soon.

Let me call your brother to come early today. You must speak today while you still can, my child. Don't lose hope. " She said. But I no longer had that hope. Everything was in my brothers' hands, but I couldn't force him to talk to me! It was time to say goodbye. I didn't like goodbyes, I never did and never will. Separation! I didn't like breakups. Up until that age I had seen many farewells. The best part was leaving without notice. Anywhere, no matter where!

Do not hold on to something that is not good for you.
Let life leave you alone.

CHAPTER
12

Time to Leave

Ms. Nalân was happily waiting for my aunt, who was also the first to welcome her home after her arrival. We were victims of a game they were playing. Was there more to say? The two stood to one side and whispered. Immediately they withdrew, they wanted to speak alone. Who knew what traps they were trying to set back then. I whispered into my Aunt Meral's ear. "We have to call my brother right away." She tried to comfort me a little by saying I'll call. Now the family lawyer Mustafa came along, and the three of them talked quietly. Every now and then I'd peek through the kitchen door unnoticed. It was reported that my brother was away. I should have gone out with my brother before Ms. Nalân and her friends found out. I could only achieve this with the help of my aunt Meral, because she thought the same way as I did. "My child, I don't think there is a way to speak to your older brother today. I think I'll have to call him again."

As promised, Aunt Meral called my brother: "It's very crowded here, you can't go out with Yasemin if you come in and they see you. You'd better not come in the house, let Yasemin come out."

Meanwhile, the lawyer spoke to an airline. *What happened here anyway? I was surprised.*

138

I entered the living room, offended. Whatever was going on, I was offended by everything and it reflected in my mood. As soon as the lawyer finished the call, he informed us. "The plane leaves at six in the morning. It wouldn't be bad if we left around two in the morning."

Something broke in me because at that moment my brother entered the house and approached the living room. "What's this big surprise? Who came? Welcome!" he greeted everyone. I went back to the kitchen and hid my tears. Although my brother had spoken to Aunt Meral, he had come into the house. The other bad news was that we were flying to Germany in a few hours.

There was no turning back, I was very sad, so I kept crying. It hurt, I couldn't help but cry. We didn't want to leave! My brother didn't know about the sneaky trap.

"Dinner is ready." Said Aunt Meral. "You haven't eaten anything all day. Let's also call Suat, you two will eat here. Your brother has come, they will not let him go."

"Okay" I sobbed. Whatever God gave, she set the table with it. I didn't really have an appetite, but I managed to get a bite or two in my mouth. After my brother had dinner we used the back door to get to our rooms. I didn't want to see anyone tonight.

We would be leaving at two o'clock, so my siblings and I would have to get up at 1 am.

Kiraz had already fallen asleep. Suat was now in bed too. After all, we had a five-hour drive ahead of us. I used the phone to call the kitchen to speak to my aunt Meral. I asked her to sadly and melancholy tell my brother that we would be leaving around two in the morning. My aunt Meral also cried on the phone. Half an hour later my brother came into my room. My mood was obvious, but I still didn't want to show it to my brother, but he understood that I was offended and hurt in every way.

"So your journey begins tonight, and we have not been able to speak. I won't keep you from sleeping, you need it," he said, kissing my forehead and leaving my room. Everything developed so quickly that I didn't know what to do. I would leave my home without having settled everything. It was like a wound that wouldn't heal. Even as the years passed, she would always bleed inside me. I felt this even then, even though I was a child. The years had passed, but the wound still bleeds and hurts.

The tape came to an end. Yasemin started crying at her last words. One of her deepest wounds was not being able to live out her childhood. It must have touched her! Who knew what else she wanted to talk about? She was originally going to send the tape she first discussed, but she immediately started recording the rest on the new tape and sent both of them to me!

It's been a long time, we haven't been able to see Yasemin for almost six or seven months. She always asked if our working days were compatible and when we came to see her.

My brother and I visited Yasemin a few days ago, the memory of her private life stayed in my head very well:

Over the phone we had agreed on a day that finally came. Tomorrow it was time, then I drove to Yasemin. I had missed her very much. We were lucky with the weather, it was very nice, neither too hot nor too cold. It was September.

During our phone conversation she talked a lot about her garden and that the other neighbors didn't want a garden, so the whole garden was hers. She mentioned that she even planted an olive tree. Planting made her happy.

As soon as we were with her, the first thing she had shown us was her splendor. "Nobody has done anything with the beautiful spot," she had explained to me. I remembered what we talked about. Unnecessary weeds grew everywhere and the property was used as a garbage dump.

I couldn't believe my eyes. She had created a garden like paradise. She spent every minute she could spare there. Beautiful, colorful flowers were everywhere. The owner had promised her that if she made something of the overgrown property, he would build her a garden house there, and he kept his promise. He had built a glass house out of wooden beams for Yasemin. "Come and see how beautiful it is," she asked me.

She had grown green beans, assorted lettuce, squash, zucchini, tomato, various spices, hot red peppers, green peppers, strawberries, cabbage, cherries, and countless more. Her latest additions had been the olive tree, a kiwi tree and an apple tree.

One side was decorated only with flowers, and only vegetables and fruit were planted on the unseen back. The front housed the grill and seating area. That day we had spent most of the time in the green splendor. We grilled and brewed our tea over the fire. We had fun until it got dark. It was a beautiful day. When we met face to face, we only talked about our everyday life. She even mentioned that she had settled into her job and started her hairdressing training at the salon she started at. These were the first steps to success. Yasemin struggled and clung to life. All the negativity she'd been through couldn't stop her from getting on her feet.

"Have you seen my relatives?" She asked repeatedly. So that she wouldn't worry, I said no, even though her brother-in-law had called my hair salon a total of six times. Even when I was shopping, he had stopped me several times to ask about Yasemin. When the time came, I would teach her gently. It was too early to tell. Even though Yasemin's whereabouts were kept secret at the time, she lived in fear, so I could not share such news with her because I would have supported her fears.

Her brother, Suat and Kiraz had come home with their hands full. We wanted to clean everything up and then follow them into the house. Time just flew by. The next morning my brother and I would start our journey home by train.

We had put the freshly picked vegetables and fruit in the kitchen. Yasemin mentioned selling nearly forty kilos of green beans and jars of chili paste. Everything was fresh and handmade from their garden. The groceries were very rare to find.

In the morning after breakfast, my brother and I prepared for the journey home. Before we left Yasemin, she gave us a bag full of canned jars from the garden with like jam, pickles, spicy paste, various vegetables and fruits.

When she said goodbye, her blue eyes lit up at me. Her head was tilted slightly to the side while she smiled and placed the small cassette in my palms, holding my hands tightly with love and hope.

Yasemin trusted me. She believed in her heart that her life story, which I was planning to publish in a book, would give hope to other Yasemins around the world and that I would help carry her story forward.

Let's see what Yasemin had to tell next, so I hit play to listen to the next part:

At 12:30 am I set my alarm. First I got ready, then woke my brother Suat and finally Kiraz, who I helped to dress. Half an hour had passed. The sounds of the floor below echoed upstairs. There were a lot of people, I could already guess who it was. Aunt Meral checked our suitcases again to see if we had packed everything. For on the go, she prepared everything we liked and put it in a bag. She held her hand over us like a mother, she was warm and loving. I was sad, very sad, but I had surrendered to fate. We had to go, it was our last minutes at home. It was time to say goodbye. Our suitcases and bags were taken to the cars.

Aunt Meral, my brother Nihat and my uncle Osman accompanied us to the airport. All victims were together. Of course, her ruse didn't go away overnight. Years later I thought how clever they were, how they got rid of us.

We arrived at the airport almost two hours early. Our luggage was handed over but there was still time to go through passport control. I had nothing more to say to my brother. If there was a chance one day I would do it. However, Aunt Meral urged, "Come on, talk!" But I was deeply hurt, not angry, I guess I couldn't be. I wasn't someone who held a lot of resentment or hatred.

Passport control was behind us. While waiting, my aunt Meral cried the whole time. Because she knew what was coming. While we were waiting, my brother Nihat gave me a sealed envelope. "Put it in your pocket right now!" He said, winking. It was our turn, it was time to say goodbye. We hugged for the last time. My aunt was a little cold-blooded about it, I couldn't feel any emotion in her.

From the inside, where the others couldn't get in, all I could do was wave goodbye. From now on we were in the care of my aunt, whom I didn't trust at all anymore because of what had happened. However, I had no choice but to seek refuge in God. It was our only shelter.

So we got on the plane, everything was new and strange. I had never flown before. My aunt packed our hand luggage on the passenger deck. 'Hold nothing. I don't want to hear any admonitions about you, there's radio silence,' she scolded us. She was cool. I had felt that before. Step by step we stepped into the unknown. Suat sat in a row in front of us with Kiraz in the middle. I sat behind them with my aunt. However, if she had a mother's heart, she would sit next to Kiraz and give me Suat. Even before the plane took off, I asked to be seated next to Kiraz. Kiraz was still young. Suat did what was necessary, but he was still a kid. But what was I at fifteen? Wasn't I a child?

I just didn't see myself as a kid at all. I never had a childhood, how sav

Sensitivity happens in compassionate man.

Yasemin's Struggle

CHAPTER
13

I was never able to live out my childhood, I didn't know these feelings of being a child. On the last shot, I was talking about what happened on the plane. The subject of childhood had distracted me. I had a hard time not crying. No, this time I'll tell you without crying. There is no cure for what had happened. We have to look ahead, only then can I progress. Since I unintentionally deviated from the topic, I will now continue:

We were on the plane. My aunt was finally convinced and decided to change places after all. So I went to the middle next to Kiraz. My brother Suat was sitting with my aunt. Since it was my first flight, I was excited. It was a strange feeling. The plane had taken off, I held Kiraz tight. Our belts were fastened. I looked at Suat to make sure his seat belt was fastened properly. It was then that I saw my aunt counting something in an envelope. The envelope had been quite thick. It looked like my envelope. They gave money to my aunt, but I didn't know who gave it to her. My brother had given me an envelope, yes, but who had given her one? This question had occupied me and I did not feel well. Not knowing what was going to happen to us, I was always in doubt and hesitant. I think this behavior was quite normal. Wherever there were relatives, I had been persecuted and harmed by them. Would these doubts increase or decrease over the course of my life? Either way, time will tell.

Germany

We had arrived in Germany. When I got off the plane, I felt that it was very cold. Joy? I had to think! No, I wasn't in a happy mood. Neither did my brother Suat. How could I be happy if I emigrated to Germany? Who would pursue the case of my brother-in-law who raped me? Who would take care of these matters if the lawyer stabbed us in the back so hard? I wanted to discuss all this with my brother, but unfortunately it wasn't possible face to face. *I secretly hoped that we might be able to communicate by phone in the next few days.* Maybe then I'd have a chance to talk to him.

My middle cousin had come to pick us up in his new white BMW. His hair was smeared with hair gel. Earrings stuck in his ear. İsmail YK's songs played in the car. I was surprised. He wasn't seated properly while driving either. Later I noticed that most of the Turkish youths who lived in Germany drove their cars in such a strange way. This bad habit had overwhelmed me. It seemed so strange for some reason. With his poor Turkish he introduced us to the places we passed as if he were taking us on a sightseeing tour. I didn't understand most of them. "Is it possible for you to tell us later, can you even concentrate on the road?" I asked. Immediately, my aunt turned me on again. Just because I said it with a very harsh reaction, she scolded me. "You dirty, rude thing.

Now you show your true face. Do you have a class friend in front of you? He's your older brother, and has anyone asked your opinion?" Yes, maybe she was right then, but he was seventeen. He wasn't allowed to drive the car unless his mother or father were with them until he was eighteen. There were rules. He behaved like handing a new stick to a lame man, like saying come on, get up and go now. There were only two years between us. However, I had been through more than he had. He seemed smaller than Suat to me. Even Suat was more responsible than him.

I respected those who deserved it and didn't give my respect to the undeserving. Of course I hadn't stared him down at one glance, that wasn't possible. Above all, by what right would I do such a thing? We weren't rude. Fortunately, after the insult, I was quick to respond: "With all due respect, he's older than me." That was the end of it. We were greeted with an argument as soon as we arrived.

I don't care what others think of me.
I am who I am.
It's not perfect, but it's real.

Yasemin's Struggle

CHAPTER
14

After an hour and a half drive we arrived at her house.

It was very old, the color from the stone, the exterior seemed to be falling off everywhere. There was a big heap of rubbish in front of the door. There was rubbish from construction and other homeowners everywhere. It took a thousand witnesses to recognize the garden. Well, it was still better than nothing. At that moment, my cousin explained. "We bought it with the money your people gave us. We just moved into this house, how is it nice?" It was pretty hard for me to answer, but I pulled myself together, I would never give up on myself. I definitely had to protect myself this time. I would also protect my siblings. Even if it was a relative, I would no longer allow anyone to oppress us. But I didn't want to appear cheeky either. As I said, time would tell.

When we entered the house with our suitcases, my aunt said loudly: "Leave the luggage at the door."

"Okay" we replied and entered the apartment on the first floor. The house had three floors, which was near the center. The upper floor was not used. There was a lot of belongings inside and outside the house from the old landlords. There was rubbish here too. I thought Germany was more orderly, I thought a lot about *how they could accept such houses.*

She said they slept on the second floor. On the bottom floor we ate and washed, there was the kitchen, the hallway, the bathroom and the living room. She said to me that they would rent it to me when the third floor was finished. How did I want to live with my siblings on the third floor? How was I supposed to rent it at fifteen? I had no income yet! However, I hadn't said anything. My aunt always spoke to me as if she were scolding. "Don't stand there, let's make breakfast, we've come from a long journey. Why are you standing there useless," she barked at me.

My uncle and aunt lived in this house with my three cousins. One of my cousins wanted to go to college which turned out to be wise, he was the eldest. Now that we were joining them, I asked in a soft voice, "Aunt, where are we going to stay?" "Let's have breakfast and then I'll take you down to your room," she said.

Sighing, I repeated. "Bring it down?" She asked. "Yes, why are you surprised, there's an empty room downstairs. Until the third floor is finished, you will have to manage below. What did you think, how could we bring you to Germany if we didn't have the usable space? Have you ever thought about it?"

Again she scolded me for asking a very simple and natural question. Her reactions were always so repulsive, harsh and cold. I couldn't understand her attitude. When I was greeted like this, it was only natural that I worried.

My middle cousin told me that his father was still asleep since he had come off the night shift. My youngest cousin was in school and my oldest in college. Since we didn't have much to talk about, I didn't even have to mention their names.

My aunt said. "Clean up the kitchen properly, I'll lie down for a bit before your brother-in-law wakes up." Not only she, we were sleepless and tired too. Nevertheless, I cleaned everywhere, as she wanted. The dishes from the night before had piled up. I had made the whole kitchen sparkle. Suat and Kiraz watched a movie with my cousin, then he came into the kitchen and we chatted a bit. His heart was pure and good, but he had nothing positive to add to himself or to his life.

"My aunt said there was a room downstairs. Our bags and suitcases were left at the entrance of the door. If you don't have any plans, should we go down to the room together? Would you please show me the premises?" I asked my cousin. He said, "As far as I know, there are no rooms downstairs." There was a short pause, then he said the word in German: "KELLER."

"What does basement mean?" I asked. Since he wasn't good at Turkish, he started to describe it to me.

"Come on, let's go downstairs while they're all still asleep," I asked him, then we went into the basement.

How would we find shelter in a place where not even rats dwelt? How would we be able to sleep in such a place? "My aunt won't let us sleep here, will she? Doesn't she have a conscience?" I asked my cousin.

"By God, what did she mean? I don't know either," he replied with great surprise. He was amazed too.

There was light in only one corridor. It was shady, even dark. The boards creaked as I descended the stairs. Also, my cousin warned me not to step on any of the steps or they would break through. The boards were damp and the whole place smelled of damp. The rooms were all filled to the brim with garbage from unused things. There was little space. In a single room, where the floor was wood, there was charcoal on the wall. There was no lamp in the room. Did they think the light from the corridor was enough to illuminate it. This is where we were supposed to sleep, on a medium sized mattress that was covered in urine, dirty and wet. There was a dirty sofa, an old motorcycle, a dirty little closet made of shelves with no doors, and that closet was supposed to be where we put our stuff? No way! I told my cousin.

I had to fight not to stay in this place with my siblings. They called that room? Enough was enough, I told myself. Every family and relatives tried to suppress us. I shouldn't have allowed that anymore. I couldn't help but start crying. "Wait, let my mother wake up, see what she has to say. Of course you can't stay here, I'll talk to her," he offered. I turned my back on him and went back up the stairs.

I remembered that well, I cried a lot. *Will I never smile?* Even rats could not live in such a place. I wasn't charcoal to tuck in there! I had to be strong and not get carried away. Before I went to my siblings, I used the toilet to wash my hands and face. Since I couldn't stop crying, I washed it over and over again. I wouldn't be able to erase my destiny, no matter how many times I washed my face, my destiny would always be the same.

When I was reasonably calm again, I went to my siblings. My aunt and brother-in-law were already awake. I was shocked but also angry, I couldn't say anything more. There was no discussion, they wanted to go shopping. *You know, I thought to myself,* that a lot of the money they got from the holding had to be spent.

After my aunt left the house, my cousin wanted to encourage me by saying. "Let's set up and clean up the first floor a bit."

With a deep sigh, I nodded to my cousin because I was frustrated and upset.

How did he want to prepare the coal field so that it could be inhabited?

After my aunt left, we spoke to my cousin. Consistent with the thought I had of him in the car when he picked us up from the airport, his heart was pure. What should he do, it wasn't in his hands that his life developed like this? The living conditions and circumstances in Germany had allowed it to be so.

Despite everything, I had come to Germany. I felt like there was no turning back. So no matter what, I had to face everything and every situation, resist everything and fight. So I had to be strong and fight against all odds.

When my aunts came back, I had to talk to her about my brother's school. Also about what I should do, maybe I got a job or did I go to school? I didn't know either, but everything had to be sorted out as soon as possible. But now I was tired, so I asked my cousin's permission to lie down on the couch. The whole night drive and the preparations made me pretty exhausted. As soon as I lay down, I fell asleep.

Suddenly I was awakened from sleep. My aunt had woken me up with such a strong reaction that I was surprised. What happened? In my sleepy state I looked around, why was she angry? Because I slept on the sofa, even though she slept too. There was a saying: "THE STRONG HUMILIATE THE WEAK!"

My uncle had gone back to bed because he was on the night shift. So I started a conversation with my aunt: "Okay, here we are! What will happen next, how will it continue? Suat should go to school, Kiraz to kindergarten and I, what should I do, go to school or to work? Aunt, what are your ideas, what did you think, what are your suggestions?"

My aunt, a little nervous and capricious, told me the whole process: "No, you put your thoughts aside. In order to be able to stay in Germany, we must first obtain your residence permit. Since all three of you are orphans, you are here because of an emergency situation. Otherwise it would have been impossible for us to bring you to Germany and your age was decisive. If all three of you had been over sixteen, the German state would have refused you entry. This is a bureaucratic country. Everything happens on paper, remains as evidence and documents. If you don't have proof, you're screwed! The first thing we're going to do tomorrow morning is go to the Immigration Office and do all your transactions.

Let's see what else they want from us. I hope that your residence permits, for one year, will be issued without any problems. "

I interrupted her: "Why only one year? What if they don't? Shall we go back to Türkiye?"

My aunt got angry again: "I said let's see, what do you expect from us? Let's go in the morning and we'll find out! After completing this procedure and getting some relief, we report back to the school and kindergarten. What is this stress? It's been busy since I've been here. Ah, shut up and let me clear my head."

I never objected or said anything. There, for the second time, I felt a coldness towards my aunt. I quietly turned around and went into the living room to watch TV with my siblings. It was a language I didn't understand, but I still stared at the TV. For the first time I stopped thinking and stared at the screen as if in a dream. No, actually like a ghost.

I wasn't dominant enough to make decisions about my own life. That's why I had given in to everything, every cruelty and injustice. Our arrival in Germany broke my arms and wings. It was like a bad fall. Despite the deliberate injustice,

I had turned a blind eye and pretended not to hear the grave insults and humiliating words. I wasn't Yasemin anymore, not the same Yasemin as in Türkiye. After I came to Germany, I played the three monkeys again because I was crushed and muzzled by everyone.

How many pains can fit into life?

Yasemin's Struggle

CHAPTER
15

Almost two and a half years had passed. I skipped what I had been through in those two and a half years. Those were horrible days.

I had pushed it aside, now it came back to me. The first night in Germany.

I kept asking myself where should I sleep? On the coal square! In this damp basement. It was dark and frigid what storms we had experienced. Those were terrible days that no one could have imagined. It was hard to remember those moments, those days were filled with cruelty.

In the summer we hunted mice and in the winter we trembled in the basement. In this darkness, in the garbage...

It was also a lie that they wanted to fix up the top floor for us. Our famous Ms. Nalân sent money when my aunt whistled, and my aunt spent the money on her sons and her home. I didn't have the luxury of fighting when we lived in the coal shed with damp walls and furniture, damp mattresses and dirt. I had no one who could stop this injustice.

My siblings went to school and learned German there. Suat was struggling, he spoke broken German, but Kiraz would be able to speak perfect German later. She could pronounce the learned words perfectly. Of course I also had difficulties.

After school I was on my way to work. Since I started working for a hairdresser as a child, I wanted to continue the profession. I ran errands. If they had given me permission, I could have started there then.

At school I met a girl from Türkiye. She was always alert. Once she said something to me that opened my eyes: "Check the length of stay on your passport. In the first five years you have to be very careful. They can no longer expel you from Germany after five years. Of course, they can identify you if you commit a crime. That depends on the size of the crime. I heard you're an orphan. Your aunt must be torturing you at home! Play the three monkeys game for five years if you're smart. Then get away from them."

She spoke very harshly, I was shocked by that. But the truth was, the girl was right. After that day, I began to live more carefully and consciously. That speech had made me a little more ambitious. It had also changed my thinking. However I stayed calm next to my aunt. I said amen to every injustice committed, I gave in because I had no more strength to fight. I was weak, succumbing to every oppression, every injustice. This was a very good trump card in their hands. Although I had a mouth, I lost my voice and ignored what I was going through.

BUT I HAD SEEN EVERYTHING!

EVERYTHING HEARD!

ALL UNDERSTOOD!

I was just tired and broken, I felt a very strong resentment. But I wasn't one of those three monkeys who didn't want to see, hear, or speak. How could a mature woman inflict tyranny on a child of her daughter's age? What was her heart? What was her conscience?

You need an ear to listen, a heart to understand.

Yasemin's Struggle

CHAPTER
16

I stayed with my maternal aunt for almost three years. In a town near Dortmund lived my paternal aunt who was a housewife and my brother-in-law was the truck driver. She mentioned being so alone. "I wish you would come to me," she would often whisper in my ear, so my aunt and others wouldn't hear.

We literally lived in the basement for three years. We even ate our food down there in the dark.

We made a fire in the garden to heat water so we could bathe in the damp laundry room. I often thought back to those cold winter days. You don't want to know how a person shivered and froze without stoves or heaters.

We had been to my paternal aunt's for the past week. Schools and my workplace were closed for three days for the holidays. If we counted the weekend, we were on vacation for five days. I had told my aunt beforehand that we wanted to go to my aunt on my father's side. My middle cousin drove us because my brother-in-law wasn't at home, he was going to Belgium. Five days felt like five hours. It had been a great time that flew by.

We felt like normal people for those few days. It was normal life in a normal apartment. It was hard to describe how

I felt that day. She gave me all the energy, power, strength, determination, fighting spirit, everything I had lost came back.

In this house I had regained all my human feelings. Suddenly I felt valuable and important. I had lived in a luxury villa in Türkiye. Everything was there from the driver to the gardener to the chef. Why did I only have these feelings now? Even though I should have had her then?

"BECAUSE MONEY IS NOT EVERYTHING! " Some things are priceless.

I had turned eighteen two weeks ago. Now I was of age. We lived in my aunt's apartment. As was customary in every household, cooking was done on the stove. But the last three years we could only cook something with the gas bottle and the tips I earned. I felt like a visitor asking her neighbor if he had an egg because she forgot it while shopping. So I hesitantly crept over to my aunt to ask for an egg. Now think of the rest...

May God let no one see these days.

When I had a deep conversation with my paternal aunt, I regained my human feelings. I even missed talking and almost forgot how to do it. You have to come, she kept insisting. Every second sentence was, come here. We could not go into other topics. When I was alone in the room with my siblings, we talked to each other about our situation. I got the answer from Suat: "Let's stay, sister, you know how we live there." So I went to my aunt to talk.

She cooked in the kitchen. She was very happy about this news. Before I even said it, I had tasted the joy. Then I hugged my aunt silently. She loved me, I knew that. "I have good news for you." I said, before I could finish my sentence she interrupted me: "You're coming, are you coming here?" Immediately she started jumping and screaming with joy.

She even left her food on the stove. She hugged and kissed my siblings. I stayed by the stove to keep the food from burning. My aunt kept dancing around the house.

"You calmed me down," she said, exhausted from dancing and jumping, then sighed again. "But my child, I have to talk to you about something. Close the door, sit here."

Immediately I did exactly as she asked, closing the door and sitting in the chair. "Aunt, speak! Just say it like it is, you don't have to be afraid." I begged her.

She was comfortable with my approach. "I spoke to your brother-in-law. He frowned, but I tried to convince him. When your brother-in-law is home, it makes me very nervous.

He always wants something. He knows nothing else. He always wants my attention from the moment he enters the house until he leaves. I can feel how exhausted I am as soon as he leaves the house. So what I'm saying is we're not used to the sound and the presence of other people at home. Maybe it'll be a bit strange for all of us in the first few days." She hesitated briefly, then she explained: "Although he is standing at the tap and could get water, he asks me to give him the water. He expects to be treated with such care! When he's at home, I always look out for him. There might be conflicts at first. We have to talk about that first, my child. I'm just talking about what could happen. Let neither you nor we live to see these days, my child. Your brother-in-law has no life outside, he doesn't set foot outside the door. He only walks the distance to work and home. That's why I want to offer him as pleasant an atmosphere as possible at home, my child.

Let me give you another example. He is so attentive that he doesn't even send me to work. I was a working lady, this is my second marriage. Sometimes the ceiling falls on my head, but there's nothing I can do. He doesn't want me to work because when I work I get tired and I can't take care of him. We've been married for four years. I want to take care of you and give you a warm home. You were born to different mothers, but your father was the same and he was my brother. It is my duty to take care of you."

When my brother-in-law was at home, we didn't go. It was good that we talked about it from the start because I liked to play with open cards. We had talked at length with my aunt. There was a smile on her face and mine now. As my siblings sat down at the table, we cheerfully and happily told my siblings this news.

It was such a beautiful, genuine, warm, happy table. My siblings were also very happy. We also brought up the subject of my brother-in-law in front of my siblings. They were silent. What seemed like a big problem to my aunt wasn't a problem for us. We lived in the dark coal shed to be invisible for three years. *What was that,* I thought at the time. It wasn't for life. The same event did not have to be the same, and there was no need to express an opinion about an event without having experienced it first. I only had this experience after this experience.

Also, my brother-in-law was a truck driver and sometimes didn't come home for three, sometimes six days. When he was home, he was only home for two or three days.

At the dining table I said to my aunt, "Nevertheless, we won't be staying with you for many years anyway. I will look for an apartment near you. As far as I've seen, Germany is a really bureaucratic country. First of all, I have to deal with the custody of my siblings that I want to apply for. I'm the eldest,

I can't endanger my siblings just to get out of my aunt's coal mine. If I get in trouble from the government, I'll have proof. She herself made us live in the coal shed. I would provide the evidence if necessary. Not for me, but to protect my siblings. They were entrusted to me by God. I have no right to betray them, nor do I have the power.

Aunt, as soon as we get to you, we have to give custody of my siblings to me by court order. Otherwise, custody remains with my aunt and she can cause us difficulties at any time. I can't even enroll in school without my aunt's permission.

Are you really ready to walk this path with me, aunt? If you say I'm in, we'll pack up and come see you next week."

"You are my beautiful niece, I don't understand everything. If you say I'm not strong enough for such a responsibility, I respect it," my aunt whispered.

"But I want an answer from you, straight and clear. Are you ready?" I asked. My aunt was very determined, without thinking, she said: "I'm in, my child!"

"Let's talk a little while we clean up. I want to tell you about other things, my child," she said. Suat and Kiraz thanked them: "We are full, aunt. The food was very tasty. Thanks, we'll go next door so you can talk in peace."

My aunt raised an eyebrow and looked at me as if to say look at these little ones. She liked that they were acting so grown up. "Yasemin, good luck, my child. You make good children out of them. They are decent and smart, not spoiled and mischievous. In addition, they are very mature and decent. You know how to behave. They love and respect you very much. Have you ever noticed the way Suat is looking at you? He looks at you like a heroine. I congratulate you on your contribution to education and your efforts. May God reward you for it.

Let's get to the topic I want to talk to you about. My child, I honestly don't know what I would do if I were you. Could I have this power? Could I be so determined to fight? Believe me I don't know. But I'm telling you, it's a shame the way they're acting. You are young, you have a bright life ahead of you. Maybe you have a boyfriend or maybe you want to start your own family later. Maybe you don't like what I want to tell you now.

You are a natural beauty. How beautiful my Lord created you, you are flawless and unique. For sorrow you do not see your admirers as they look at you. I know you care about your siblings, but you will never have a life of your own. You know that, don't you? You will never have a free life of your own. Maybe someday when they go their own way. Only then will you have a life of your own. Will you be able to hold out until that day? Can you endure this? When others build their houses and start their families and you see their happiness, won't you be depressed, my child?"

With her words, my aunt had led me to another realm. I was distracted. It played like a movie in front of my eyes. Never having been asked such questions, I murmured my next words: "No." But it was not a clear and decisive answer, because what my aunt had told me I had never considered before. In other words, I had never thought about it until this day. But I wasn't able to think about these and similar topics anyway.

When my aunt then realized that I didn't want to deal with this topic, she steered the conversation in a different direction.

"Yasemin, what I really wanted to tell you was, there are many reliable facilities for children. You give your siblings to the family you want. You present your terms, if the other party agrees, a contract can be formed. Once they have taken in such a child, you have no more problems. You decide the range yourself and you can even visit your siblings in their families at any time. You can meet up with your siblings whenever you want, you will always keep in touch with them. The decisions are made together. There are such institutions and families that accept such conditions. Until you build your life. You get a job, you buy a house or you rent an apartment.

You arrange your furniture and then you take your siblings back in. How about we go and talk to a facility like that?

"No way!" I said harshly, but not disrespectfully. My aunt spoke up without overstepping her bounds: "Okay Yasemin, we're closing this topic for good." We were both quiet, and after clearing the table and cleaning the kitchen, I opened the door. "You can come" I called my siblings over to us.

Immediately Suat and Kiraz came in. "Now that we've all made our decisions, let's tick off Plan A. Let's go to plan B. In order to realize this joint decision, we will implement Plan B. How do you think we should do that?"

"We'll pack our bags and go on Friday after school." Suat said.

I agreed with my brother.

"Suat said it well. I think you should do that" my aunt said.

"But we can't just go and leave the house with our suitcases. That would be too noticeable. It's best to take a suitcase with me to work every day so that it doesn't attract attention. Suat knows where I work. He then brings Kiraz from school to my work. Together they can wait for me until I finish work.

Our adoptive parents had another adopted son, aunt. He had put money in an envelope for me at the airport before we came to Germany. I opened the envelope and looked inside. At first I thought it was a letter. When I saw the bills inside, I immediately closed the envelope again. I didn't count it. I don't like to travel in the evening, especially when there are children and you live in a foreign country, you can feel the danger beforehand! We must protect ourselves. That's why we come by taxi. I'll see how much it costs. I know for sure it will exceed two hundred euros and I'm sure I won't have a two hundred euro tip by Friday. Since this is an emergency and difficult situation, I'll take the money from this envelope. I'll put it back in the envelope. If something happens to me, you put the money you took back in. This envelope will find its owner!

My revenge will be terrible! "

My aunt was quite thoughtful: "I wanted to ask why you want to put it back, but your last sentence says it all. Don't take a dime out of the envelope. I'll pay the cab when you get here. Don't worry about it " she said.

I absolutely did not accept this offer. "So far I have not harmed anyone financially or morally. I'm someone who can get by on my own. It's not my harm, it's my advantage. Check here for schools by Friday. The two children have to go to the school office if necessary. Inform yourself already. Let no trouble come upon my siblings. If need be, let's hire a lawyer."

We had discussed all aspects. My aunt said she would take care of the school and custody applications until we arrived. I was relieved about that!

Now it was time to go back to the darkroom. Thanks to these human and loving moments that we shared with my aunt, I found myself and became stronger. From now on I wouldn't close my eyes anymore, I was strong and powerful enough to fight. It was really good that we stayed with our aunt for the holiday. I found myself, I was happy and ready to fight against oppressors and injustices.

How some people manage to put up with themselves,
remains a mystery to me.

Yasemin's Struggle

CHAPTER
17

The next five days passed quickly.

The holidays were over and we were groping around in the dark basement again. We had now spent two and a half years there.

Our things, which were shipped from Türkiye to Germany in a container full of goods, are used by my maternal aunt for her sons and for her own house. All bikes, big and small toys, furniture, whatever was in the container. We hadn't seen anything of it since that day. What she couldn't use, she sold or gave away. Everyone will one day be held accountable for everything. I have great faith in the righteousness of God.

As you read these lines, there may be people who think I'm ungrateful. Does it exist? No idea! I don't know, but let's pretend. I am by no means an ungrateful person. I will not forget the good or the bad. The reason we wanted to go was an aunt who caused suffering to her nephews and family. We witnessed terrible atrocities in that basement.

Those who are still alive will feel my vengeance. That's probably all I can say on the subject.

My paternal aunt wanted to take care of the court applications immediately. She gave us the documents she had prepared.

The pastries and some wraps she made for us were wrapped. "You don't cook, that's enough for two days." She said. I was overjoyed with her gentle manner, since nobody had thought of us like that since our aunt Meral. This approach was good, she gently caressed my soul with it.

Back in the coal room, in that nightmarish place where we spent our endless nights in dark rooms, I began to make preparations to leave this family, who refused even a greeting from God, even though they saw and heard us coming. I'd said to my siblings. "Pretend nothing happened."

We continued to live as before. My focus was that this topic was definitely not up for discussion. They had to understand the seriousness of the situation. Maybe I was too hard, but only because I loved her. Only unity would be strong, otherwise we could not fight together. So we just held hands to give each other support.

We were now ready to fight.

There was no more Yasemin to bow before others, neither did Suat and Kiraz. From this day to this day, no one will be humiliated in front of anyone, and there will never be the three monkeys who did not hear, see, or speak. I would never succumb to this injustice again, I had to fight. So that my siblings would not bow either. I had to be strong. Now that I had reached that age, I was old enough to protect my siblings and myself. I wasn't little Yasemin anymore.

As a young person who, by the age of eighteen, had already seen life hit rock bottom and had unwanted experiences, I was smarter and more mature than my peers. The light of my life was extinguished when I was raped at the age of thirteen by a mature man of thirty-seven. "Don't do it, uncle. Don't do it, uncle... let me go!" I begged him. The light had gone out as I begged these sentences helplessly.

What kind of life are we talking about here?

Did we write about my life that didn't exist? Oh god, did you laugh about this situation or did you cry? I was actually surprised too. Should I laugh or cry about it?

We wrote and quote my life that didn't even exist. I never found a place in the leading role. What a strange event! I would like to share a special thought in small pieces with Nurgül who was listening to my audio recording!

"Nurgül, you know. I could always be "myself" with you. That Yasemin you know is actually me. But some people don't know me like you know me. Maybe it's better like this. The one or those who saw me hurt me. So I built a wall around me to protect myself. This wall protects my siblings, not just me. You became a part of me, even though you saw my insides you didn't hurt me. On the contrary, you held your wings over me and opened your door. What I'm going to say is while I was talking about my life that hadn't existed a moment ago, this came to my mind;

Wow, writing is a talent. I don't think everyone can write. Writing isn't for everyone. I recall emphasizing this again;

"My life was darkened, extinguished, when I was thirteen. When I was raped by the thirty-seven-year-old man that I called Uncle.

My feelings are devastated, my heart is numb...

Th I came to the conclusion that you were talented enough to make a novel out of my nonexistent life. That's a talent. To find something that has been lost seems strange. I may not have been aware of it, but you gave me back my life that I didn't have and was dead. I can't thank you enough! Yes, you gave me the life that was taken from me!"

Let's pick up where we left off:

First I had to wash our clothes. The weather wasn't very hot so I washed our clothes as soon as we arrived as they were difficult to dry. Although there were exactly two washing machines and one dryer, I heated water in the garden by lighting a fire. I hand washed our clothes in the garden even though there were bathrooms on the upper floors!

Meanwhile, my siblings did their homework. Suat taught his sister to read. That's how we survived this day, there were still four days left. Every day I went to work with a suitcase or a large bag, so for four days I gradually took our belongings out of the house. I would leave nothing behind and I would not settle for little.

My revenge would be mighty!

Thoughts like revenge were normal now. It was as if Yasemin had disappeared. The deaf, blind, mute and nodding her head suddenly no longer existed. During the holidays with my aunt it was as if I had become a completely different person. My ideas, my thoughts were no longer silent. This Yasemin was different now. There was no mercy for those who showed no mercy. Torture for those who did. Yasemin, who could not harm anyone before, would now harm herself. But certainly not to those who were without guilt or sin. Finally I could distinguish who deserved it and who didn't. I was in tune with myself again. This Yasemin wanted revenge. Everyone should dress warmly from now on. Feelings of hate and resentment formed within me, they should pay for the wrongs this world had done to me. These involuntary thoughts scared even me.

That's how we survived the next three days. We carried on our dark lives like rats in a small coal mine, as if nothing had happened. If you call it living and that in the heart of Europe!

It was Friday, the excitement of stepping into the light was in our hearts. Everything went according to plan, everything was fine. Since they never came down, they didn't notice that our belongings were getting fewer by the day. But if we took them all at once, it would have been noticed. Our plan unfolded as it should. On Friday morning we left the house with my siblings. By the way, I gave my siblings another bag when we left the house. Their load was heavy, but I had made the right decision to consider taking a cab. Without experiencing any emotional moments, without looking back, we set off as if nothing had happened. My thoughts were warm, like the sun rising in our hearts, the light, the sun, the deep blue sky. Like I'm on my way to liberation.

For three years we were buried in darkness. In that moment I understood better the survivors of a prison. Now I understood why they took deep breaths when they left the prison because I did the same. Breakups usually hurt me, but now I didn't feel a thing as we left. Filled with emotion, pain and sadness, I didn't even look back.

My paternal aunt called my place of work. I had no money to buy a cell phone. Since I had to use my tips to buy groceries and necessities, there was not enough money for other things. In fact, we experienced an absence of existence.

When my aunt said everything was fine, I was so relieved. I had also said goodbye to my employer. He gave me my salary until the last day. He was a good person and compassionate, he even said to me. "Come on, get your bags ready. Treat yourself to another coffee, you don't have to work until the end of the day. When your taxi comes, I want you to leave without stress."

I thanked him very much. We stood in front of the hairdressing salon with all the suitcases and bags. I hugged my siblings and waited for our taxi. In that moment I was strong. There I decided once again to protect my siblings and to build a wall around them. I fervently asked my Lord to give me power, strength, perseverance, patience, mercy and love. So that they wouldn't have the experiences I had gone through. This thought gave me a lot of strength.

I looked lovingly at my siblings, they both continued to wait calmly in my arms. "As long as my Lord gives me this power, I will always be by your side like a guardian angel. I will protect you from evil. You will be useful people for the country you live in. You will be polite and decent. As long as I'm with you,

I hope nothing will happen to you. Your sister has rebelled since today, from now on those who do harm shall fear us!"

I made that promise to my siblings that day. I hoped my Lord would not stray me from my path!

We were out and very excited. Our journey lasted almost two hours. Kiraz fell asleep for a while with her head resting in my arms. I was so grateful to my Lord at that moment!

When we arrived, my aunt was waiting for us at the window. When she saw us, she immediately ran to us. She kissed and hugged us, then tried to carry our luggage. I was shocked. She wanted to pay the taxi driver. But I had already given him the money before I got out. When that day came, I would put it back in that envelope, and that envelope would find its owner.

No one is worth losing your smile.

CHAPTER
18

Hello New Life

My aunt cooked various dishes and set the table. At that moment we were happy, as if we were celebrating our liberation struggle.

It was a four room apartment. A small room and a children's room were empty. We hadn't used the children's room because they had put their household items in it. In other words, an empty space was used as a storage warehouse. When we arrived, there were three beds measuring 90/200 in the room that belonged to the three of us. To make it a little more comfortable for us, she had laid out a new carpet, renewed the curtains, arranged the quilts and pillows nicely and there were beautiful flowers on the windowsill. Our aunt had prepared a warm room for us. The other empty room was smaller and actually my aunt would have prepared this room for me if I wanted to, but I never thought about sleeping apart from my siblings, I couldn't take my eyes off them yet.

I hugged my aunt gratefully...

I had to take a deep breath because we were in our new life. We got rid of the darkness: "Hello new life, hello!" I said with joy. My brother-in-law came home in four days. That was good, so we could unpack everything and settle down.

He shouldn't see our hurry, we had made this agreement with my aunt. That's how I wanted to keep my word.

Now we could have discussed the problem with my maternal aunt. We should have paid attention to this issue before my brother-in-law got home. We should have taken it seriously. If I took the wrong stance, the state could take my siblings away from me because I didn't have custody. So I shouldn't have been bad with my aunt and shouldn't have caused trouble until I got the title. I had to act very logically and wisely.

Very resolutely I told my aunt on my father's side that I wanted to call my aunt on my mother's side. My aunt was nervous but I was able to silence her and bring her to her knees with one leap because I knew a lot. My aunt was very surprised when she heard that. But that was the truth!

So I called, it was my middle cousin who picked up the phone. "Hi! It's Yasemin," I said.

My cousin asked: "Yasemin, have you bought a mobile phone? Ha, ha, ha, or did you put new power lines in the basement, lady? Yasemin, seriously, your siblings didn't come home today. And where are you, where are you calling from?"

He paused for a moment, he was silent and waited for an answer from me... "Listen to me carefully, I have to talk to my aunt, it's urgent. If she's around, could you give her the phone?" I asked.

'She was just here, she's upstairs now, my mother isn't with me. If you find yourself in a difficult situation, please tell me immediately. Let me know, tell me while my mother's gone,' he begged me.

"Definitely no! I need to talk to my aunt urgently. Could you give her the phone, please?" I insisted.

"All right! Don't be angry, I'll bring the phone to her! You strike me as very strange, Yasemin. I'm feeling weird right now. Let me get her the phone, give me a minute!" he told me.

"Thank you," I replied.

"Hello Yasemin? Where are you, where are you calling from? Didn't you come home? Tell me, what's so urgent?" she asked.

"Aunt, we're not coming back. We left the house this morning. We won't be back," I informed her.

"Girl, do you know what you said? Do you know who you're talking to?" she snapped.

"Aunt, please, please don't interrupt me. Let's talk like two adults without arguing. Without blaming each other. We must now look ahead. We can't find common ground by fighting each other! We decided not to come home anymore. Accept that peacefully?" I admonished her.

"Of course I don't agree, what a crock! You come right back the way you left. Otherwise I'll complain to the state, they'll send you back to Türkiye," she threatened me.

"You threaten me and you've silenced me since the day I arrived. I always bowed my head next to you. But that's not the point now. You don't need to be angry. We were already very useless people to you, so you didn't care about us at all. You're not even upset that we're gone. It turns out your generosity was just self-interest. What if I tell you that I know that Ms. Nalân gave you a lot of money? I would not tell Ms. Nalân that I left you. You get the money into your account and continue. I won't tell them anything. You neither! You're enjoying that money now but when the time comes I know how you're going to throw up the money. That you took from us to feed your family. If you don't bother me, nothing will happen to you. But don't worry if you cause trouble. My revenge will also have great damage for you. Let me tell you this from the start.

Now I ask you again. Will you voluntarily accept our departure without causing us any difficulties?" I asked.

Confused and stunned, my aunt breathed, "Yes, I agree."

"Okay, that means we understand each other! I'm glad, then you'll get a letter from my lawyer the day after tomorrow. In it, you declare and sign that you have given me custody of my siblings and that you are doing this voluntarily. You will send it back to my attorney immediately. Don't follow me, I have no time to lose, aunt," I said seriously.

"Agreed, my child," she replied.

"Good that makes me happy. So I hope we keep in touch. Goodbye, aunt," I said goodbye.

"Goodbye, Yasemin," she replied.

My paternal aunt had listened to our phone call with her mouth open because I had put the phone on speakerphone and recorded it. Maybe I didn't sign it and send it back, thinking she was going to cause trouble. Even though I knew it was a crime, I had made an audio recording to have evidence in my hand to protect myself.

A few minutes had passed but my aunt was still staring around. She was very surprised when I spoke to her: "Aunt." Then she looked at me ...

"Are you afraid of the Yasemin I was on the phone?" I asked.

"I was frightened, yes, my child. That Yasemin isn't you," my aunt said, still confused.

Yes, I accidentally scared my aunt. But what brought me into this situation? When you think about what I went through, what persecutions and tyrannies I went through. What nightmarish nights had I experienced? What about my lost childhood or my life that was taken from me? Who would pay for this? I harbored thoughts of revenge against the people who let me experience this at the time, and frankly, it scared me myself. On vacation I had discovered a new Yasemin in myself, a stronger one. It is with great ambition that I protect this Yasemin in the hope that I will fall into the hands of good people. Only good people saw me like that now. No one will be able to crush, humiliate and oppress me. From now on, an expanded Yasemin stood in front of them. I will take my revenge on every single one. This was my firm decision.

That was the first time I got up that day. I wanted revenge on all of them.

My aunt relaxed a little after I talked like that. It was a relief for me too that she understood more clearly why I spoke the way I did. Because I had only just discovered this Yasemin. It was a new feeling for me. Yasemin, whose personality was being warped, could not even raise her head and answer, even when being tortured by her aunt. I couldn't even say a sentence in front of her. If I were strong, no one could torment me. I've always said that and I say it over and over again. Like I said, I felt stronger now.

By now we had eaten. It was quite late, so while we talked, my aunt and I packed our bags, cleaned and then went to take a shower. It was exactly twelve o'clock that evening. It was good that the week came to an end. We had some time to recover. Early Monday morning I had to do my transactions.

If you don't tell me what you want,
you won't get it either.

Yasemin's Struggle

CHAPTER
19

In the morning, right after waking up, I had brewed the tea. How I missed making tea on the stove. Of course I was quiet so as not to wake anyone up. I calmly prepared breakfast. First Kiraz woke up then my aunt. Suat must have been so tired he was still asleep. We started to have breakfast. As we sat around the table, we started talking to my aunt about how our lives should go from Monday onwards. So that Suat and Kiraz could not interrupt and continue their schooling, I contacted the schools they were to attend and informed them that we were moving. My aunt had even petitioned the court for custody. Suat would start his new school on Wednesday. It was also very close to my aunt's house, only two minutes away.

My aunt enrolled Kiraz in school before we came. They were lucky and would have told her: "There will be a vacancy in a month, we can take her in after that." I urgently needed to find a job for myself. First of all, I had this custody issue in front of me. If I hadn't snapped at my aunt like that on the phone, she would have used and tormented me again. From now on everyone got what they deserved. My compassionate feelings seemed to be diminishing every day. Of course, this change made me think a lot but it was a change I couldn't control. I had only embraced this personal change through the bad things that had happened to me.

My aunt asked, "Shall we go out for a bit in the evening? You'll get used to it as soon as you look around." She smiled, then added, 'We're in the middle of the city.'

So we decided to fix up the room my aunt had allotted us together. While we were setting up, everyone gave their opinion on it. In the end we had combined the two beds. We put the other one in the unused little room where the closet was. We had suddenly made the decision that Suat would get the small room on his own. Kiraz and I would sleep in the same room. We were all happy with this decision.

After lunch, washing up and tidying up, it was time for the evening excursion. Then suddenly we all got up to leave. I felt free as a bird, I was peaceful and happy. With that peace and happiness in my heart, I looked to Suat, Kiraz and my aunt.

"Kamen is a clean, small and orderly town," I said as I strolled through the little market. The shops were all closed. The only thing that was open were the catering establishments such as kebab shops, pizzerias, bistros, cafeterias...

We strolled comfortably further through the city into smaller alleys. Suddenly I read a sign in front of a salon: "Hairdresser (employee) wanted"

I was very happy that I had found the job advertisement. I immediately said to my aunt: "I'll come here on Monday and introduce myself."

After a long walk we were back home. My aunt said let's drink hot cocoa, that would warm us up. So we drank hot chocolate while watching movies in front of the TV. Somehow we had all arrived at the right point. The seat was very comfortable, wide and huge. We also had our blankets with us. Oh, I said at that moment, come, my sweetheart, come please! My aunt and I fell asleep lying down. That's how we experienced our second night.

Sunday was spent a little quieter in the house. In the evening we had unpacked the remaining suitcases, made the beds, cleaned and organized the house. We were all determined to go to bed early. We would have a lot of work to do from Monday, so we needed to be freshly rested and were going to bed by nine o'clock.

In the morning after an energetic breakfast we all got ready and off we went. First we went to an appointment with our lawyer. He wrote a letter and sent it to my aunt. That's why I took out a loan from my aunt in the first few days which I wanted to pay off as soon as I worked and earned my first money. Even if she didn't take it like she said she would, I would leave it somewhere in her apartment. I didn't want to be a burden to anyone and I won't be. This is one of my principles.

The attorney enlightened us, "Don't apply for custody in court unless you hear from me." So I did exactly what my attorney said and waited!

Right after the lawyer we went to the hairdresser. "Hello, are you looking for staff? My name is Yasemin," I introduced myself. Then I had a conversation with the owner of the salon where I talked a little bit about my past. At first he was a bit skeptical about my work permit but then he was relieved when I proved to him that I had a work permit. "Come to the rehearsal tomorrow and we'll see," he said, smiling. I smiled back and said, "Oh, I'd love to!" Then I left his salon.

My aunt accompanied me and we went home very happy. After that we didn't have much to do.

"Even if they pay you under the table, take this job Yasemin," my aunt advised me. Without thinking, I replied, "Oh no, why should I accept it? My pension, insurance and taxes should also be paid into. I'm sure of what I'm doing. Why should I lower my value? As a newcomer to Germany, why should I cheat the treasury? NEVER… An employer who appreciates my craft will also pay the value I deserve."

My aunt gaped at that answer. It wasn't even a lie!

The doors that seemed closed every day were wide open. My inner and outer world became brighter by the day. To be honest, we didn't have a casual relationship with my aunt. We had a very respectable, sincere, warm and mature relationship with one another. Everything went well now.

I wondered what it would be like when my brother-in-law came home. The thought crossed my mind. Then one night as we were all laying under the covers watching TV I said,

"Hi guys, are you asleep?" They were all breathing softly, nobody said a word? "Huhu to everyone here, hello? I just remembered something," my voice echoed around the room.

Suat and Kiraz sighed and snorted. My aunt gave a start: "Oh Yasemin, I was asleep! What's on your mind?" She tried to get up from the couch slowly. I woke them all up.

"My brother-in-law is coming tomorrow. So far everything has been very good. We have never made excuses for our manners, demeanor, respect and reverence. We have to abide by the terms and rules of the agreement we made before our arrival so that nothing happens. Guys, we won't be hanging around when my brother-in-law gets home. We will always leave the house spotless. We'll be useful, okay guys? Now you can go back to sleep," I said. After saying what I wanted to say, I could continue watching TV with peace of mind. Satisfied, I leaned back on the couch and crawled under my covers.

Then I thought about my new job. Tomorrow I would say hello to working life again. The salon owner had said to me, "I put up the ad last night, we took it down early in the morning." So it was all luck. If God grants, He will open the door of sustenance for you. But if my Lord does not grant, you cannot get your livelihood. Oh Almighty Lord, grant us what is good for us! (Amin) I prayed quietly inside.

If they were satisfied, they would offer me a full-time position so I could get a normal barber's salary. As I sat on the couch and thought about it, many goals came to mind.

I wanted to learn karate with my siblings so that we could defend ourselves. If necessary we would even take private lessons, I had risked everything. After that, no one would be able to push us around. You don't fight violence with violence but with intelligence!

My first trial day went very well. My employers were happy too. They saw that this girl's hand was quick and dexterous. They made me work all day, then shamelessly asked, "Are you coming to rehearsal tomorrow?"

I answered confidently: "I was here all day for a rehearsal. Are you happy with my craft?" "Of course, thank God, we all like your style of work," my boss replied. I came to rehearse one day. They were pleased with my craft. So what was the purpose of the second day of rehearsals?

So in the end we agreed on a full-time position.

"I don't know, I don't understand, I don't want to get paid under the table or anything," I explained. Afterward he said, "You're quite open, clear and tough. It's good, I like the way you are because I don't pay under the table," he said. "I'm just being principled," I said.

"Well, then start at the beginning of the month, bring the necessary documents with you," he urged me. It was almost a week until the end of the month. That day my brother would also come to school. In the morning I would take him to school until he got used to it. Everything went according to plan.

It was evening and my brother-in-law still hadn't come. My aunt had been in a hurry all day. There was a hectic excitement at home. She had reflected those emotions onto us in such a way that I understood the seriousness of the speech at the time. My aunt was in a panic before my brother in law came home. She had prepared everything perfectly. "Was he like the way she talked about my brother-in-law?" I was amazed. Was his interest that great? The first day, the first encounter and the first evening would tell everything. I had always prayed that we would get through this day too.

Before my brother-in-law came home, I saw extraordinary changes in my aunt. She had changed a lot but I left her alone. My brother-in-law had been calling twice a day since the day we arrived and he had texted my aunt on occasion. He also welcomed us home over the phone with happiness and joy.

My brother-in-law called. "I'll be home in forty-five minutes," he informed us. He always called ahead. My brother-in-law came, the door opened and my aunt walked around the house as if she were only there to serve.

"It's your home from now on, don't be ashamed, children," he said. But if he actually said the things he didn't want to say, he would have put us in danger too. Deception was the worst thing there was. That's why we all need to be open and clear with each other at all times, no matter what it was. Otherwise, we may unintentionally endanger and harm other people. I had thought a lot that day.

A wise man once told me, "Let people do what they want so you can see what they would rather do."

CHAPTER
20

Finally, my brother-in-law arrived. My aunt had filled the bathtub with foam like she always does. She had prepared all my brother-in-law's new and clean clothes, towels, even his music. *It meant that every time my brother-in-law came, he took his bath first. Now, why was my aunt so worried about my brother-in-law?*

So that everything happened according to the agreement and regulation of the house, we stuck to it.

First, my brother-in-law greeted us all then he went into the living room. Before he sat down on the sofa, he invited us: "Come on, everyone. Let's sit for a while." So we all went into the living room and took our places.

My brother-in-law said to us: "Children, welcome. Thank you for coming to us and feeling this place is right. You have sought refuge with us, we will not leave you alone. We stand behind you. Relax, everything will be fine. You will lead a regular life here. As long as you believe in it, you can achieve anything."

I then explained that we didn't want to disturb his order.

"Thanks for everything, brother-in-law. Suat goes to school. A month later, Kiraz starts school. Well I found a job. Everything will be fine, brother-in-law, I think so too!" I replied.

After my brother-in-law went to the toilet, I cleaned up the table. I kept admonishing Suat and Kiraz, "Don't stand there and be quiet if you can. Let's not disturb my aunt's order." I didn't want to do that, because that's how we had discussed it, not to disturb her peace and her daily rhythm.

There were many conversations around the table that day. My brother-in-law didn't ask many questions, my aunt had warned us beforehand. She told me later that she warned him, "Don't overwhelm the kids with questions." I sent my aunt and brother-in-law into the living room after dinner because Suat and I wanted to clean up the kitchen. We had also made the tea and after they both went into the living room we had tidied up and cleaned both the table and the kitchen. Now and then Suat would come into the living room and freshen up his tea. I had already put Kiraz to sleep.

It was about nine thirty in the evening. We wanted to go to our room and asked permission. That night Suat slept in the same room with us. For the first time I could pick up a book and read it. Although I love to read, I hadn't had the opportunity to read a book in the last few months. I picked up the book that my late adoptive father gave me as I have not been able to finish it. But from that day on, I was determined because I believed that I would lead a settled life. So I read the book through in one go.

Maybe I had missed something, because it was the first day, what my aunt had told me was too much. It would be clearer in the next few days. That's what I discussed with Suat: "Let's wait and see."

The next morning I woke up to Kiraz combing my hair. Suat was still asleep. The voices of my brother-in-law and my aunt reached us. My aunt was in a hurry again, she was running around the house so early. It was Suat's first day of school so we woke him up and got ready with Kiraz. After that we went to Suat's new school which was very close by. In this way he was very lucky. Of course Suat was very excited because it was his first day of school.

When we got home, my aunt was still in a hurry. My brother-in-law always wanted something from my aunt. She couldn't even sit still and had changed a lot. She seemed different when my brother-in-law was here and different when he was gone. When my brother-in-law was away, she was warmer, more genuine, and more loving. Now she was grumpy and she laughed out of necessity. I didn't think my brother-in-law was like that.

After three days, my brother-in-law was back in the truck. So we were home alone again. I still had a few days to start my new job. I was happy about that, my hand would earn bread again.

"When I start to work, I'll move into our own four walls with my siblings," I said.

"No, it's too early. The state doesn't accept that. You've been here for three years. You have to live with someone who already has a residence permit here for five years in order to get your residence permit," she explained. "They won't let you rent your own apartment yet. You can cause unnecessary trouble. You work these two years, save your money for yourself then it is easier to rent an apartment. Then you can earn your living. You have responsibilities, needs to be met, expenses to be met. You have to think about that too. It's hard being single alone. Save your money first. Settle down here first, then you can think about your own four walls and make it happen."

She was right, in that moment I agreed with her.

Flowers grow as they are watered,

unless hopes are given up.

CHAPTER
21

A few months had passed. We had been living with my aunt for almost three and a half months. Suat got used to his school and made new friends. He began his schooling with Kiraz and immediately learned the German language. I also commuted to my daily work. Because of my job and talking to customers, I had also started to speak more German. I now understood everything that was said but of course I had difficulties speaking it. Kiraz and Suat were well understood, they spoke without a dialect. It was assumed that I could get by in Germany but the truth was that to this day I have had my difficulties.

My salary was good. For my work I received one thousand two hundred euros net. Added to this was an average of fifteen to thirty euros in tips every day. I gave my aunt five hundred euros a month from which she bought the needs for Kiraz and Suat.

One day my aunt asked me: "Actually, you get monthly child benefit from the government, but your aunt will probably still receive the money. Have you ever asked her?" I had no idea about the subject. So I called my aunt and told her about it. Although we hadn't lived with her for four months, she hadn't brought up the subject. After some time we had the child benefit transferred to our own account via a lawyer.

In the meantime, she had signed the custody agreement for my siblings, which my attorney had sent to my aunt. Now I had been able to apply for custody of my siblings in court.

In the beginning I was able to set aside seven hundred sometimes nine hundred euros a month. After all, my tip and salary were very good. I didn't have a lot of expenses.

After the sixth month I was able to save one thousand five hundred euros a month. The money I had saved on the side had given me a lot of self-confidence. As I said, my revenge would be very difficult. For those days I saved my money and prepared myself. We continued to go to our karate training regularly.

The situation of my brother-in-law and my aunt was really as my aunt mentioned in the first few days. My aunt was in an extraordinary panic before my brother in law entered the house until he left the house. In the meantime my aunt was also exposed to the violence of my brother-in-law. It was impossible for us to intervene in this situation as long as she didn't make a sound herself. When my brother-in-law was home, it was obvious that my aunt was under pressure. When my brother-in-law was gone, I tried to talk to my aunt many times but she wouldn't even talk about it.

When my brother-in-law came, we tried to stay in our rooms as much as possible. Eventually it got so bad that we took Suat to our room for a short while because I was worried. But it didn't do us any good. I wish my aunt hadn't either.

After a certain time, I gave my aunt all the rights. I understood better and more clearly why she was in such a hurry. My uncle was actually a psychopath. Despite everything, my aunt had depicted and described him as rather boring.

The house phone rang. While my aunt was on the phone, she suddenly started crying. Apparently she had gotten bad news. As soon as the call ended, my brother-in-law, seeing my aunt sobbing, cranked up the music and asked my aunt to dance. But my aunt wasn't in the mood to dance because she had received a death notice. My brother-in-law had hit her very hard for not doing what he asked. I remembered it well, we locked ourselves in the room until my brother-in-law left the house. We hadn't eaten or drunk anything during those two days. It may be bad to say but we even had our needs taken care of in the room. If I had gotten the slightest signal from my aunt, I would have done my best to intervene but she never gave me that signal. My brother-in-law had also hit me a few times for defending my aunt. After I was alone with my aunt, she ordered me: "Don't interfere, I don't want it, don't defend me. In those moments you take your siblings and lock yourself in the room." How many times had she warned me but after a while she still got very angry at my interventions.

On the days my brother-in-law was there, I told my aunt to pretend we didn't exist. How many times had I told her to ignore us.

You don't need to listen to a person's screams.
You can read his life with your eyes,
hear it with your mind, and feel it with your heart.
Just want to see and hear.

CHAPTER
22

We spent almost a year in the same apartment. During this time I had saved a lot.

Without telling me, my aunt saved a hundred euros each month for my siblings. One day she said to me: "Take this money, my daughter, EUR 1,200 for Suat, EUR 1,200 for Kiraz. From the money you gave to the household, I saved a hundred euros per person for the children. But don't leave that money with me your uncle may see it. You can keep it if you want. You can also open a savings account. Instead of giving the household $500 a month, you give $300. I put two hundred euros aside for your siblings."

I was surprised about that, actually I was happy about it. In fact, she spent the remaining three hundred euros I gave her for us. It wouldn't be okay to live at their expense.

Our karate classes became more intense as we took private lessons from our trainer. We received highly professional training and continued our education regularly. Suat passed his class and I continued to work. It was a very nice and well-attended hair salon. Business was very good. During this time I had won many customers. I've had clients who specifically wanted me to do their hair care and updos and inspiration was plentiful. People came from far away who wanted my updos and bridal hairstyles. Word got around very quickly.

At the weddings there were no fewer than ten or fifteen people with me. My boss was very satisfied with my work and my craft. So he even started giving me a bounty for the updo and bridal hairstyles. "It's yours!" he insisted. I had a good and loyal boss. He worked in a company and was not a hairdresser. It was weird at first but over time I got used to it.

My boss was the greatest. He and his siblings were orphans like us. They had lost their father seventeen years ago and their mother fifteen years ago. It was a wound that made their hearts ache and filled with sorrow. But life went on with its good and bad moments. As the eldest, he felt responsible for his siblings. He had taken care of his three other siblings over the years and never married, thinking there would be trouble at home then. He didn't even intend to consent to the marriage. He had already completed this page.

Once he said to me very seriously: "Never forget that. You are not alone when you get into trouble, remember you have a partner in destiny here. As a team and family, we always have your back! "

Those words gave me a lot of confidence and strength. His youngest sister also worked in the hair salon after her hairdressing training. Two sisters and two brothers, two married and two single.

When I first started working, his sister bossed me around. My boss immediately intervened in this situation. He was a merciful boss, although he was very clumsy and disciplined. Not once had he patronized us and the workers had not abused this goodwill. We all embraced our work as a team. "I'm a worker too, that's our bread and butter," he always said very modestly.

In the company he worked for, he now worked twelve hours a day instead of nine. Sometimes he couldn't stop by the salon so he let me do the daily checkout, not his sister.

One day he stopped at the hair salon at noon when we had few customers. Though he had no positive thoughts about the second partnership, he said he had no other choice due to time constraints. A week later he had walked into the break room with a man I had never seen before. However, our chef would never bring his special guests to the hair salon, he would say, "Those whom I wish to entertain I do not entertain at our bread source but either at my home or to a good meal at the restaurant." They were up to stayed in the back room for a break. As we had just finished the hair salon, the two stepped out and our boss introduced us to his new partner.

To be honest, I didn't really like the guy. He looked us all from head to toe but we would still get to know him, it was necessary not to have prejudices.

From that day on he stopped by the hair salon every day. On the first day he came as soon as we entered our workplace. Without looking at us, he spoke to us: "It's time for a cup of coffee." Then he sat down at the cash register. He hadn't made a good impression on us. Even though he was the boss, we didn't want to take everything he said. Suddenly I blurted out, "As you can see, we're all at work. "You'll bring my coffee as soon as you're done, young lady, " he said commandingly. "Outrageous, disrespectful, cocky!" I thought, very angry.

For the first time, I felt like I had pushed my limits, like it made me a different person.

Instead of saying anything, I kept quiet. *So I made him a cup of coffee and took it to him.* After drinking his coffee, he wandered through the hair salon. Now he also accepts payments from customers. We didn't even go to the cash register. He was in the salon every day, from morning to night. Either way we were at work.

Eventually he started bringing his acquaintances into our break room, who used to sit in the back room where we took our break. We ran out of space to eat our food. While they were in this room we could not go in. We could have entered but we didn't want to.

Now and then our old boss came into the shop. He seemed to understand our situation one day and after work called me on my cell phone where I had spoken to him very respectfully and accurately about all the negative changes we had experienced at the hair salon. The rest was up to him but I had to say it. From every single pin that fell to the floor, he should know what was going on in his salon. We thanked them and then hung up.

My colleague was about to quit her job because he had humiliated and bossed her around a lot. One day after work, our boss met us to talk. In the end, he admitted to us that day he made the wrong decision. He had a foreman position in the company, as a mechanical engineer. He explained that he didn't enter the partnership because of his distrust of us but because of his inability to be in the salon as often.

Things weren't going well at work anymore. Every day he came into the store with a grumpy face. So we all sat down, including his partner, a week later after work and talked openly. After that there was some calm.

After opening the hair salon in the morning, I heard voices coming from our break room. I saw that his partner had brewed the tea, coffee and breakfast. But he couldn't make up for the mistakes he'd made, I thought.

"Good morning!" I greeted him. I hadn't thanked or flattered him for his preparation. As I set down my bag and jacket to enter the salon, I saw an empty liquor bottle under the sink. "What! Do you drink at work?" I asked him. I saw that the new partner was hungover because he could hardly stand. "You're damaging our workplace," I accused him, his incompetent behavior no longer having any limits. As I turned and walked out, he came from behind, grabbed my arm and turned me towards him.

"Remember, honey, you snapped at me! Pray for your blue eyes, your black hair, otherwise I would already have you in my hands. Is there someone in your life?" he asked. As he said these things to me, I struggled to free my arm from him. "Let go of my arm!" I repeated over and over. He said he only let go so I wouldn't raise my voice even more.

Day by day his greed increased. Whenever I entered our break room, he would come after me. He always had an eye on me when I was working. Working there was no longer good for me because I no longer felt safe and vulnerable. One night after work, he followed me home and called after me. I immediately contacted my old boss and voiced my complaint. "Okay, I'll talk to him," he replied.

If nothing changed, I would quit my job like my colleague, I explained to him. "Something will change, don't worry!" my old boss promised. After that I really trusted him and believed that after this conversation something would change.

About a week later, as recess approached, my boss's new partner and I were in the salon. I was dealing with my last client. As soon as the customer left the salon, the door was locked from the inside. We'd always done it that way, it wasn't strange behavior. After the final cleaning, we opened the door, left the salon and locked it from the outside. I usually went after the daily cleaning.

Actually, two other colleagues were still present. It was school day for the trainee, a hairdresser was ill and my other colleague had resigned because of these incidents. My boss's sister finished work at five o'clock because she always left at five o'clock because she worked in shifts. That was their agreement. As always, when it was too crowded, I stayed here alone.

In the beginning I worked from 9am to 8pm on weekdays and from 8am to 6pm on weekends. My working hours were quite scheduled. Of course I also had my day off. My boss was a fair boss because he paid all my overtime. Even my salary was increased when the hours changed. He now gave me €1,500 net plus my daily tips and the pin-up bonuses.

I was making good money but I had to quit my job because of this fanatic who called himself his partner.

All eyes were on me that day. I worked like I was on guard. I didn't feel good at all anymore. All day I felt like something was going to happen.

I also had to put away the dishes before leaving the break room but I didn't want to go inside. Actually, I wanted to finish the work in the salon earlier and leave immediately. But I couldn't leave the chaos like that. Long story short. He followed me as I walked into the break room and got ready for the end of the day.

"Come on, let's have a coffee somewhere. There will be a change, we will share two words. We'll get closer and let each other feel warm," he said. Instead of speaking to a person who didn't understand the word "NO", I preferred to leave the hair salon as quickly as possible but he blocked my way.

"No, no, no... I'm in a hurry, I have to go home right now," I then yelled at him.

"Okay, let me drive you home today. Let's break the devil's leg. Let the ice melt between us, you'll see, maybe we'll get along well! What do you say, little lady? " he asked.

I quickly walked to the outside door, put the dishes down and grabbed my jacket and purse. The key wasn't on the door, while I looked for the salon key in my purse, he continued, waving his hand where my key was lying: "Little lady, are you looking for your keys?" I stubbornly asked for my keys . I frantically knocked on the door from inside to attract the attention of passers-by. Since the hair salon was closed, I had turned off most of the lights.

"Hop young lady, what are you doing? Stop banging on the door, you'll round them up." He admonished me, but I didn't stop. In fear and panic I knocked on the glass door of the hair salon. When a group of young people noticed me, he said, "You don't understand jokes either. I was only fooling. Come on, you gathered the people in front of the salon. I'll open it, I'll open it, don't keep hitting, oh! " So he opened the door and gave me back my keys.

He smelled like alcohol, I was disgusted because I hated it. I came home crying. I immediately told my aunt everything. "My daughter, call your employer immediately, tell him everything. Come on, have a sip of water first, calm down my child. Then call and tell him. He needs to know what's going on. Wow, that bastard. He will never forget this day! I'll tell your brother-in-law so he can see it's not a joke" she said angrily.

However, I insisted on not telling my brother-in-law but she told my brother-in-law anyway because she thought what she was doing was right.

After I calmed down a bit, I called my boss and said that unfortunately I had to quit my job. He was surprised at that! He was at work and said he would call me as soon as he retired to the office because of the very noisy environment.

I was still upset when he called. So I told him everything that had happened. Of course he was very angry! "Don't worry, I'm out of a partnership now. Be at work tomorrow like every day, Yasemin. We'll use our trump cards, no question!" he replied.

"From now on, I'll only come back for my things once and I'll be right back. If you can, be at the hair salon in the morning," I said. I remember crying until I fell asleep that night. How nice we all were at work before his partner came into the salon. We worked peacefully together. Ever since he came, he had upset our entire working atmosphere.

My boss was there when I came into the salon in the morning. He immediately called me into the break room to talk to me. That's how I went! He must have come early, the tea was already brewed.

"Good morning, Yasemin. Before we begin, I would like to express my sorrow for yesterday. Believe me, I'm so sorry. I don't know what to say. I'm thinking about wishful thinking but unfortunately it's no use. We had a fight with him yesterday. He threatened me as soon as the conversation started. That means I got into trouble without even realizing it. Bread is such a great scourge that it affects our household. Rest for a week or two if you wish, don't make a hasty decision. This is your workplace. I don't want you to lose your job. You take care of your siblings, you need money. You won't believe it but we had a terrible argument with him yesterday. Hardly anyone spoke. He was rebellious and he constantly snapped at me, cursed and threatened me. In order for him to leave the partnership, I have to repay his investment. It will take some time. I hope there's no further damage to the salon before then," he told me. In the middle of our conversation, the salon window glass was suddenly broken.

The entire window glass of the hair salon fell to the ground with a terrible sound. There were broken glass everywhere. He immediately called the police. In the middle of the drawing room lay a huge stone. When the police arrived at the scene, he told the police everything that had happened. Since it was morning, the only witnesses were an elderly couple. They also didn't want to testify because we're foreigners. "We didn't see it!" they claimed. They later told me in a mall that they had seen it but since we were of foreign descent, they didn't want to come forward as witnesses. They were afraid because they would have to face him face to face. That's literally what they told me. But wasn't a witness a witness? Did it matter what your ethnicity was?

Without evidence that it was him, the police could not charge him. After all the important and necessary work was done, my boss immediately called a camera system company to install cameras.

A contract has been signed with the company. The insurance company was informed so that they would cover the repair for the new glass. After sweeping away the broken window, we headed back to the break room. I offered my boss that I would wait until the insurance company and the glazier came.

Inside, I gave my boss my written resignation which I had written with my aunt the previous evening. I took the vacation days that I had not yet taken up to the day of my termination. So I had almost six weeks off with paid overtime.

"Stay here until you find a job. Don't be stubborn! You call the police as soon as he gets here, they'll come right away. Don't quit your job!" he begged me.

But I was very determined I wouldn't go back. I really felt sorry for him. After a brief farewell, I returned home. I worked there for a year and a half, that's how long we lived with my aunt. Time passed so quickly, it flowed like water down the river.

As always, when I got home, my aunt was in a hurry. It no longer felt weird when she didn't take my offer of help. So I told her I would go to my room and lie down. As I lay on my bed, I cried a lot and slept a little. With so much accumulated inside me, I couldn't stop crying for days. By the way, my brother-in-law had come and gone for two days. The night before he left he asked me to come in while he was watching TV. He wanted me to tell him the story. At that moment I looked at my aunt and my mouth twisted slightly as if to say oh why did you say that.

"Tell me about that bastard who hit on you. Did he bother you more than you told us? How lucky you are, people who come and go depend on you. How unhappy you are! If you had a man with you, no one would look at you sideways! You are young, beautiful, charming and well-groomed. Well, you just moved here, you got a lot of attention. All eyes are on you. Open your eyes. Look around you with a buyer's eye," he urged.

Before my brother-in-law finished, I immediately interrupted him. He had gone too far with his words so I showed him that I didn't like his ways. "I don't want to talk about it any more," I said, and asked to be allowed to retire to my room.

My siblings watched TV in the room. After sitting down between them, I put my arms around them and we watched TV in silence that evening. After a while Kiraz lay asleep on my leg. Suat, on the other hand, was lying on the bed and looking out from the bed. I carried Kiraz to her bed, after covering her up, I lay down on the sofa with a blanket. As I stared blankly at the TV, my mind went to the words my brother-in-law had said. "What was he thinking, talking to me like that?"

I was very nervous, it was very difficult for me. He wanted to drive again at night and when I got up in the morning I was so glad not to see him. To be honest, I didn't know if I would be able to hold out much longer here in this apartment. If he had said it nicer, I might not have felt so offended. How he talked to me like he'd slapped me in the face. Even his gaze was very strange when he said those words. Every now and then while I was watching TV, his evil eye would flash before my eyes. I shook my head, wanting to erase those eyes from my memory as quickly as possible.

When we woke up in the morning, I had an argument with my aunt. Why did she say it. She was also in a strange state. "I didn't think your brother-in-law would talk like that. You know, my intentions weren't bad. Your brother-in-law's words were difficult, I know you're hurt," she said very innocently. In any case, it shouldn't have happened, but it happened!

My brother-in-law wouldn't come home for seven full days. This time there was a tour through Germany, Belgium and France. It was great when he wasn't home for seven days..

The truth is bitter, the truth hurts.

Yasemin's Struggle

CHAPTER
23

Some time had passed and things had calmed down. My aunt and I went to the employment agency to report my unemployment. They said I had to apply, they would pay me 60 percent of my salary for a year. After I submitted a written application, my salary was transferred. In the meantime, of course, I wasn't idle, I was constantly looking for a job. To be honest, I didn't want to work too far away.

One day my aunt said, "I wish you had done your professional training. It would have been better for you. That would give you security. You'll see, maybe you'll be enrolled at a master's school after your vocational training and can do your master's certificate. Everything is in your hands. Not every employer can pay as well as your old boss. Think carefully about what I said. I think you should see the value of this job!" It was a good idea and I thought about it. Then I confirmed to her that I felt it was right.

After consultation with my aunt, we decided to go back to the employment agency. I had explained that I wanted to do an apprenticeship. I was given a list of hairdressing salons offering training. At home I went through the list one by one. I left my phone number and application at every salon I went to.

Two days later, a call came from a hair salon. They invited me to the hair salon to talk. I went there that same day so as not to lose any time. We talked and agreed to do an internship until the start of vocational training. I was very happy about that, at least I would still be working instead of being idle. The salon I chose was a German hairdressing salon. It was better for me, I learned the language faster that way. These new developments had given me a lot of strength again, I was motivated through and through. "You start with four days a week," she explained to me. Sure, why not, because I was willing to start an internship beforehand.

However, I had to earn and save money in order to take revenge on those who had hurt me one by one. I slowly began my preparations. Through the internet I was able to track who was doing what and what condition they were in. My first target was the famous Ms. Nalan. I knew many of your secrets!

Seven days had passed and my brother-in-law was home again. We tried not to walk in front of his feet as much as possible. My brother-in-law had become a complete stranger, as if he hadn't been my brother-in-law then and is now a stranger. At least I noticed the change. If I had been able to legally rent a house with my siblings back then, I would have moved straight into our own apartment. But since I wasn't allowed to do it for those five years, I couldn't use that right. *Whatever the rule,* I didn't understand why they still wouldn't allow it.

Every time my brother-in-law left, my aunt would throw herself onto the sofa first and a deep "Oh!" would come out of her mouth. It was exhausting for my aunt because she couldn't sit at all, the propeller kept turning in circles. After my aunt threw herself in the chair, I sat down next to her. Of course, whenever possible, I wanted to have an in-depth conversation with her. Her ability to perceive depended on how tired she was! I had a feeling that something would change now.

I started talking to my aunt seriously: "Nevertheless, I wish you hadn't told my brother-in-law! Something inside me says that after that day there will be changes in our lives, which is not positive. My brother-in-law had never looked at me like that, not once, until this day. But that day, my brother-in-law looked at me very differently. I could see that change in his eyes. I saw that difference in his eyes. Why did you still put me in such a situation? Okay, you didn't do that consciously. You approached this subject with good intentions. That's why I can't be angry, I can't be offended! I hope that this feeling inside me won't come true. I hope I understood it differently. But if my feeling is right, I'll take my siblings and leave immediately, even if the three of us have to sleep on the street!"

As I spoke, my aunt straightened up and sat down. She gave me her full attention without interrupting me. She always saw me as a mature person because she respected me and what I had been through. Therefore, the dialogue between us was smooth and strong as everything was done with respect. My aunt was very quiet. Even though I'd finished speaking, she was still sitting stiffly across from me, looking into my eyes.

Suddenly I couldn't take it anymore. "Don't look at me like that, say something," I urged her. She was still staring me in the face. What I said made her think. It took her a while to recover. It was like someone suddenly coming to their senses, just like that. Suddenly she turned her head left and right, then shook her head.

"My child, my beautiful niece! What you said is very bad. I couldn't believe it while listening, it was too bad to think about!" she confessed.

That answer told me everything. My aunt could have interrupted me too, "what do you think about your brother-in-law. He would never do such a thing." Look, she couldn't say I was wrong! If she had said that, I might have felt better and more comfortable after that speech. But unfortunately, that answer, which she gave in her stunned way, actually got me thinking. I had no choice but to hope it wasn't.

The wound opened in the heart never closes.
It only connects the top to the shell.
The mark underneath remains intact...

Yasemin's Struggle

CHAPTER
24

I started as an apprentice with the new hairdresser and got to know the author Nurgül, the author who had made my voice heard. I want to talk about how I first met the one who wrote my life from my point of view. I want you to know what I went through, how I felt and my own opinion from my point of view. The first day I started, Nurgül's first sentence was, "Oh my god, how beautiful you are!" Actually, I thought the same thing when I first saw her. She was warm, reliable and sincere. She didn't ask me questions about my personal life like others do, only about my work life. Of course, I later learned that she thought she could disrespect me and my life by invading my privacy. A nice thought! Not everyone can think so carefully. I was very interested. After the little chat we had at that first meeting, I wanted to know more about her.

During the briefing, my boss explained: "First, until the customers get used to you, pay attention to our working style, look at our working techniques, stand next to us and observe the customers. Watch, watch." "But I know everything," I said. She then added: "Yes, I know, but our customers are a bit strange. New ones are not accepted immediately. Of course you can take over the customers who accept it. With the others, you watch us at work." That's how I'd used it.

When Nurgül worked, I usually stood next to her and watched her. Although my boss told me to pay attention to the techniques and working style they were using, I had tried to analyze Nurgül by observing them closely. But she wasn't aware of them. If she listens to this recording, she might be surprised and say to me, shaking her head, "Ugh! Yasemin, what have you screwed up again?" While she was listening to this recording, I wouldn't be there. But if I analyzed it well, I was hundred percent sure that it will be like this. Anyway, maybe we can read that from her later.

Many things went through my mind as I watched her work and tried to analyze it. She loved laughing in a safe environment. She was a respectful, genuine and warm person who knew her place. *Who was she? How was her life? What did she do after work? Was she married? Did she have children? It had been a few years since she moved here, I overheard a client talking. Where did she live before and why was she here? Where was her family?* These questions kept running through my head. I really wanted to know. But since she respected my privacy very much, I didn't dare to ask some questions. She was a very principled and disciplined person.

The hours that she was in the salon, the boss didn't have to keep an eye on the salon. Nurgül was always in the salon, it was almost as if she was running the hair salon. I meant she was doing her job! She was a diligent hairdresser. From time to time I listened to her conversations with the customers, I had listened more closely to specific topics. I was interested because she was very close, very genuine and very warm but despite her approach, she was still distant. She was the only person I knew who had such a high regard for privacy.

Although she looked pretty tough and strong on the outside, her shoulders were hunched and her heart was tender. From the outside she looked like one ready to break but she was fragile. So she actually built a wall around herself. I realized that day that she hid her inner world and built a wall to protect herself.

In the evenings, just before closing time, a young man in his twenties occasionally came into the hairdressing salon. As soon as he entered the salon, Nurgül left everything behind. "Welcome, my dear, my very dearest," she greeted him. "Oh God! Oh God!" For the first few days I had thought that she had such a young lover. I was very surprised when she later called him "Oh, my little one, my baby". But I couldn't hear what they were talking about because at that time my work was taking place at the other end of the drawing room. He always came at the same time as the evening cleaning.

One evening he'd stopped by before she left work. This time our boss, Nurgül and this boy started joking and laughing. Our boss said: "You see, your brother is right." Sometimes they also had brief conversations from time to time, for example: "What should I cook for you tonight, my little one? What do you want?" That really piqued my interest.

Again, during a conversation, I learned that they lived together. *So she lived with her brother. Since she called him my little one, she had a close bond with him. So we had something else in common.* She took care of her brother and mothered him for years. In that moment I had felt such warmth, closeness, trust and respect for her that it was unspeakable. That day she became more precious in my eyes and in my heart. Whatever happened, it was on that day that I decided that I wanted to be closer to Nurgül. Actually, she had interested me since day one. I wanted to know more about her but it hadn't worked.

Touch someone's life so it touches someone else's.

CHAPTER
25

Our daily life went on the same way. One day, when my brother-in-law came, I pretended to my aunt that I was ill. So that I didn't have to leave my room so I wouldn't run into my brother-in-law. And then I suggested to my aunt, "If my brother-in-law is coming, why don't you guys go out? Go to restaurants, to the movies, shopping, walking, shopping again, I don't know what. Why are you always at home?" My aunt replied happily: "You're right!" She tried to convince my brother-in-law. He would see through my illness role after a while, so I put on this fuss to get them out and make us comfortable.

So I reserved a table for both of them in a fish restaurant and bought their cinema tickets. Then I booked a wellness hotel for two days. It was a bit pricey but they didn't get anywhere else. That's how I got through the next few days that my brother-in-law was at home. He was scary to me now, I didn't trust him. His funny looks stayed too. As I realized I was right, I withdrew a little more each time.

There were friends and relatives as few as the fingers of one hand. They were the only ones and I was very happy when they came. But I was uncomfortable breathing in the same apartment with him when they visited me!

One evening my aunt and brother-in-law went to the Christmas market with their family friends. Anyone who lived in Germany knows it was something special. I loved Christmas markets from day one. "Finally we are alone with my siblings in the evening, we relax," I thought and after a long time we had a peaceful evening. Kiraz had already fallen asleep on my lap while watching the film, it was ten o'clock at night. She actually went to bed early on weekdays and I don't mind if she stayed up a little late on weekends.

I took her in my arms and laid her on her bed, covered her up and walked away quietly during the commercial break. Under separate covers, Suat and I continued to watch movies.

Knowing they wouldn't be back early allowed us to be comfortable. It was after ten o'clock. The movie we were watching was over and then we were watching a new movie that was just beginning. During the Christmas period they showed very good films. I understood most of it now, I had learned German well and my tongue turned around the letter R much better. Before my aunt left, she said, "We'll probably be home by twelve or one." I had done everything I could to avoid confrontation. This time I wanted to be in my room at exactly twelve o'clock. That's what I asked Suat too, because when my brother-in-law got angry at home recently, he also started yelling at Suat.

Now my brother-in-law started to show his true colors. It was another seven months before the five years were full. Of course, I felt compelled to be patient for another seven months but then he would soon feel my revenge.

Shortly before twelve, Suat and I retired to our rooms. "Don't make a sound, get under your covers now, little one," I said, kissing his forehead before closing his door.

I immediately retired to my room. Kiraz was fast asleep, I put on my pajamas and lay down next to Kiraz. I lay awake in bed for almost an hour. My aunt still hadn't come, at some point I fell asleep.

In the middle of the night I woke up to a squeaking noise. I didn't move at all, lying on the bed with my back to the door. The door to my room was open and someone was looking in. The lights from the other rooms shone into our room. The shadow of whoever was standing in front of my room door was reflected on the wall right in front of me. It was my brother in law!

I lay still, my eyes slightly open, watching the shadow fall on the wall. I was scared It was the first time I woke up at night and witnessed such a sight. Until that day I had never woken up. I went to bed at night and woke up before my alarm went off. That was my sleep pattern up to this day. With a thousand questions running through my head at that moment, Kiraz shifted in bed. When he saw something moving, he wanted to close the door. But when he saw that Kiraz had just turned around, he continued to watch me. I didn't know what time it was, I had to turn over to see it and I couldn't turn over in bed or he would notice I was awake. They were scary moments for me but also repulsive and disgusting.

From the shadows you could clearly see how he began to caress his chest and stomach with one hand. My brother-in-law watched me sleeping outside my room door in the middle of the night and came for a treat. Then his hand went lower and lower. As he masturbated, I began to hear his breathing. After a while he quietly closed the door from the outside. I couldn't handle that.

He was dishonest, mean, and ruthless. I was his wife's niece, what a shame he had done. Stunned, I wanted to jump out of bed.

Suddenly I heard a violent argument between my aunt and my brother-in-law. But I kept a low profile and I felt as if I had my hands tied to the bed. I experienced moments of fear, it was a nightmare.

In the dark, I stared at the ceiling with my eyes open, then sat cross-legged on the bed, put my elbows on my legs and covered my face with my hands. I remembered staying like that for a while. That night I couldn't sleep until morning and put my brother-in-law on my revenge list. I would take my revenge on every single one of them. The time of my revenge drew nearer by the day.

In the morning I had pretended not to know anything. Today my brother-in-law left again. As always, my aunt told him her weekly plans. She would text him what she had forgotten, or tell him over the phone. Either way, she would definitely say it. So my brother-in-law knew when my aunt was home and when not. Sometimes, when my aunt wasn't home, my brother-in-law used the house phone to call. I usually wanted Suat to answer the call. When we hadn't noticed anything, Suat brought the phone to me and let me call my brother-in-law. "We can't see each other, niece. Did you get used to it, how are you? Let's see more often when I come back. Lately we're either going somewhere or there are visitors in the house. I missed you," he suddenly made such or similar speeches.

As soon as my aunt got home, I informed her, "My brother-in-law called to say hello." "Did he call home?" she asked curiously.

"Yeah, he didn't know you weren't home," I replied. "You mean he couldn't reach me on his cell phone?" she asked thoughtfully. "Still!" I said, raising my voice a little at that moment. "I said you weren't home, he ignored it. He told me what I just told you, I said. And you say he couldn't get through to my cell phone. For God's sake, please think clearer," I huffed, sounding a little hard. My aunt was still unresponsive.

This was not a prejudice based on an assumption, but a fact that came up four or five times in a row. After the fourth and fifth experiences, it's normal for me to have this view because I wasn't wrong. Of course I could be wrong but since day one that thought and feeling hadn't led me astray. On the contrary, it was a fact of how many times I wasn't wrong.

So I warned Suat not to bring me the phone. Especially when my aunt wasn't home. "She's lying in bed, sweeping the stairs or has gone shopping," he was supposed to make up excuses.

There were only three or four months left until I got a permanent residence permit. Until then, I had to somehow get through everything.

I regularly searched the Turkish Internet. I was constantly busy with the project and the organization of my plans to make it come true to get my revenge. My revenge would be very painful.

I had thought of everything down to the last detail.

It was a Sunday in December! My aunt had a date with her friends that day. Luckily my brother-in-law wasn't at home, he had told my aunt beforehand that he would be back on Wednesday. Suat wasn't home either. He received special training from our karate teacher so I was home alone with Kiraz. After resting for a while, I thought about communicating comfortably with my contacts from Türkiye.

We had decided not to cook that day. My aunt wanted something to eat when we met and I said to Suat, "We'll order pizza when you get back from karate." That day we had freed ourselves from the hustle and bustle of cooking. It was very difficult to rest during work and due to responsibilities. I wanted to use that when the opportunity arose. Kiraz played alone. So I wanted to take a nice bubble bath and filled the tub. I put a skin mask on my face with relish and sat down in the tub. Then I turned on some relaxing music. My body was tired, it was necessary to rest from time to time. I stayed in the tub for almost forty-five minutes, then got up and while I was lathering my hair, I heard a noise in the bathroom. I immediately washed my face, pulled aside the curtain that was covering me and looked to see what that was. All I saw was the door closing at that moment.

Anxious, I called out to Kiraz several times. When I heard nothing, I turned off the water and called her again. She answered a little later and then I continued to wash, relieved. While soaping my hair for the second time, I heard the sound again. My hands, face, hair, head and body were covered with foam. Immediately washing myself under water, I tried to see something again, my eyes stinging from the foam. The door closed again but I still couldn't see anything. To be honest I was scared! If Kiraz came in she would make a noise, at least she would let me know that she was coming. She would not walk into a room unannounced without waiting for an answer. Despite being small for her age, she had no such habit, Kiraz wouldn't go in anywhere. So I was both afraid and distrustful of this situation.

I quickly washed off all the foam with clear water. Wrapped my hair, then me, in a towel. I immediately went out without taking my clean clothes with me. In fact, I always got dressed or changed in the bathroom because I'd never been in the habit of walking around the apartment with a towel.

On my way to my room, my brother-in-law came out of the kitchen unexpectedly. At that moment I cried out in fear and my hands clutched the towel tightly. I hastily passed him and rushed to my room. He didn't take his eyes off me, even as I rushed to my room. Until I closed the door from the inside.

Actually, my brother-in-law wasn't supposed to come until Wednesday. He had not informed my aunt or us of his arrival. Of course he knew that my aunt wasn't home, she had a date. He also knew that Suat wasn't home. His coming was pre-planned without saying anything to anyone. Luckily Kiraz was in the room. That calmed me down a lot. She played with her dollhouse without being aware of anything. Exasperated, I asked Kiraz, "Did you come in twice while I was washing?" "No, I didn't," she replied. So my brother-in-law saw me naked!

"I wonder if he stood by the door and watched me?" It was sickening to even think about the situation.

I got dressed in a hurry, half backwards, half straight, because I was totally beside myself. We had decided not to leave the room until someone came home. My brother-in-law kept calling me. "When you're done, Yasemin, come and cook for your brother-in-law. I'm hungry! " he shouted. If I went out it was a problem, if I didn't it was a problem too.

"I'm hungry, when is my brother coming?" my sister kept asking, making a face. Despite wanting to get out, I started playing with Kiraz and her dollhouse. In less than two or three minutes Suat came home, then we also left our room.

"I thought you wouldn't leave your room," my brother-in-law snorted. I answered in passing: "I had work to do." I had secretly told Suat, "We're going to have dinner at the pizzeria. I put on Kiraz. I'll be right there, you'll get ready too!" As soon as we were done, we informed him, "Brother-in-law, we're going out, our aunt knows." Fleeing, we closed the front door behind us and ran down the stairs as if we were running away . My hair was even still wet. I tied her up with a scarf in case the weather was too cold. As we sat at the pizzeria, I called my aunt to tell her that my brother-in-law was at home and we didn't get home before she returned from their meeting. My aunt was immediately concerned: "Has something happened?" "Don't stay too long," was all I asked her because I wanted us to go home with her. "Okay!" she said hastily.

Within half an hour my aunt walked into the pizzeria. She hurriedly sat down next to us. "What happened, what happened, tell me?" she asked me to speak. "It's okay, I wasn't comfortable at home, so we decided to eat here and didn't want to go home until you came back. Thank you for coming immediately," I replied.

Actually, my aunt reacted correctly but she was unable to intervene. I still didn't understand why she was tied up like that. I had a hard time understanding it!

I was very satisfied with the hairdressing salon where I started as an intern. Nurgül immediately noticed that I was sleepless and exhausted from time to time. She tried to cheer me up when she had time. However, she didn't know what was going on. It was private. Because of the German Christmas holidays, the hairdressing team always went out to eat. It was my first participation, I wore a very elegant and simple, black, tight dress which reached to my knees, I had done my hair and put on make-up. I was very careful that day. When my brother-in-law saw me like this, he didn't let me go. He was very angry with me! He even took my cell phone from me, which he did every now and then to see who was calling me, he checked me out. But if he didn't find anything, he returned it. In order not to argue, I let him. But he wouldn't let me go, I couldn't cancel the meal, although a seat was reserved for me. The food was pre-ordered. I didn't leave my room until the next morning. I cried a lot, it was very difficult for me. If I were someone who went out a lot, I might be exaggerating. But I had never really been anywhere until this day.

The next day at work in the hair salon, I apologized and said some reason why I couldn't come. "Why didn't you let me know?" they scolded me.

Actually, I wanted to be honest, but I didn't want to talk about my family problems. We got along well with our colleagues and I had gotten used to my new job. After the internship, I was very happy to hear that I could start my career with them and I was very determined because I didn't want to spoil it for myself.

Life is full of surprises.
If it's white today,
there's no guarantee tomorrow won't be dark.

CHAPTER
26

It was Christmas! In the year 2008.

Two family friends were invited. I couldn't get out of the kitchen that day. First preparing the food, then cleaning the kitchen kept me busy. Then came New Year's Eve, the two or three days had cost us a lot of strength.

The visitors arrived, all splendidly dressed. The table was set and they were in a good mood. Of course I had promised my aunt that I would take care of the service. Because I wanted her to take care of her guests. In the meantime, I wouldn't be able to be with them much. My brother-in-law and other guests started eating and drinking. There were Christmas entertainment programs on TV. The joys were there and the conversations grew darker as time went on. After the dining table was covered, I had prepared snacks, fruit and a variety of hot and cold appetizers and arranged them nicely on the table.

The drinking scene continued. The second raki bottle was opened and glasses toasted one after the other. I didn't like this drink and the drinking environment at all. It reminds me of very bad times.

After I went to the kitchen to clean and do the dishes, my brother-in-law came over to me. He stood in front of me, running his tongue over his lips. "Give me ice cream,

Yasemin!" the creep demanded. He took every opportunity. When I saw him, I immediately turned my head the other way. I was disgusted with him, he must have felt it for sure.

"I'll bring in the ice cream, you can go to your guests," I said. However, he didn't take his eyes off me until I walked out of the kitchen. There was still an hour and a half to twelve. I had to pass the time for an hour and a half. As I paced in and out of the living room, he immediately gave me his attention. My aunt got up and danced in a mood to dance. They were all very happy and their morale was good. It was like I didn't belong with them.

By twelve o'clock they were all outside. So I use the time and was able to continue cleaning up. There was only the kitchen to finish and I was immediately involved in this work. After cleaning I wanted to retire to my room. It was a very busy day.

When they came back in, they continued to enjoy themselves and drink. After my aunt had two glasses, I asked her for the keys to my room. Because the key wasn't in the door. "In the box in my room," she replied, but she was unable to handle it or bring it to me. Despite my perseverance, my effort was in vain. I had already put Kiraz to sleep. Suat would also sleep in Kiraz and my room that night. Finally we retired to our room. The three of us lay on the bed and fell asleep in front of the TV.

In the middle of the night, when the guests must have left, we could hear my brother-in-law and my aunt talking loudly from our room. It was unclear which room they were in. Because this echo was reflected on me as if it came from every room. Sometimes they talked to each other like they were screaming and sometimes they talked to each other holding their voices up. This conversation was so loud that they woke up Suat and I at night. Suat went back to sleep after a while but I couldn't sleep because I didn't feel comfortable at night when my brother-in-law was there because I didn't feel safe and didn't trust him. That night I had to force myself not to sleep until I heard no sound from either of them. No matter how tired I was, I shouldn't have slept because they were both drunk.

Again, I lay with my back to the door, which is how I usually sleep. Their voices had become a little more subdued. From time to time my eyes closed, I had a hard time that night. But for my safety, I shouldn't have slept.

That night the door was suddenly opened again. The light from the other rooms cast shadows on our wall again. I lay there frozen because I was afraid! Even though my two siblings were with me, I was scared. I had relived that frightening scene again.

From what I could tell from his shadow, my brother-in-law was watching me outside the door and stroking himself again. Suddenly my aunt saw him. "What are you doing at the door?" she asked in surprise! My brother-in-law quickly withdrew and quietly closed the door. Suddenly he started arguing with my aunt. Their argument was very loud and that night he hit my aunt several times. My aunt, as she always did, remained silent. Now I was finally awake. But in a way it was good for my aunt to see that scene too. She finally realized I wasn't wrong.

In the work environment, Nurgül noticed that I was always afraid of sudden movements. In those moments when I was afraid, she reassured me: "Yasemin, darling, don't be afraid! Why are you afraid, my little one, only we are here. You don't have to be afraid of anything, you're in good hands here. Don't worry!" It was a warm and very friendly demeanor of hers. Who knows, while she'll be listening to my audio recordings, she'll surely smile at that part as she reminisces about those days?

I was a very shy person, even if I saw someone standing next to me, I was scared and immediately jumped up. But luckily I survived those days. Today I felt strong. They couldn't destroy me, couldn't bring me to my knees, despite their blows and every stab of the dagger. I had fought, so I was always busy struggling. I fought against those who had wronged me. At that time everyone wanted to destroy me, they couldn't do it. I fight! I was very down in this war against the bad guys. They accused me, I was slandered, pushed, beaten, despised and humiliated. Over the years nobody had given a drop of love for me. I was stolen from love. I noticed the good or the bad right away, should I say it was life experience? Still, I could be wrong about one person, after all there were good actors among us.

Maybe my struggle wasn't over yet. Although I think it was over. Maybe I should keep fighting. After all, we don't know what we'll be tomorrow. Only God knows! How can we get up and think for ourselves or make plans for tomorrow when we don't even know what's going to happen in two seconds? We are ignorant servants, forgive us!

The difference between then and now is this: Looking back, I feel stronger now. I intervene, I fight those who have wronged me. I can no longer be suppressed. From now on, I bow to no one. I have two siblings that I had to be strong for. So I had to fight for them, too. Two have been entrusted to me by my Lord. Maybe my exam was twice, maybe my Lord honored me to take care of my two siblings. Who knows? I want to complete this test, which totally honors me, for God!

Part of me was filled with love and compassion, the other part of me wanted to wage war against them. I wanted revenge! I want revenge in a way that didn't cost anyone their lives! My revenge drew nearer by the day. Soon it was time, I will soon drown them all in the dark. Even though I was far away, I knew them all. I hadn't completely broken off ties with Türkiye, I had my people there. We all prepared in our own way for the time when my revenge will begin!

When my brother-in-law came, we were under a lot of pressure. Added to this pressure was the harassment. Fear spread over us. Suddenly he was in front of the door. Without prior notice; like the days before... Especially the days when he knew I was always home alone. In the days when he knew my aunt was not home at the time, he looked for an opportunity to be alone with me. I felt his thoughts. His eyes meant everything. I was in his dreams and fantasies.

His facade was now completely gone. He no longer had any sense of shame. He had even touched me when we happened to be walking past each other, giving me a hungry look. I was disgusted with everything and everyone. Now that the danger was present, I understood once again that I could not stay in this apartment.

I only had a few months left to get a residence permit. I wish I had had a little more patience! To this day I had not understood what that law was. Why couldn't I rent my own apartment five years ago? It was a bureaucratic country, everything was orderly and disciplined. Would Germany ever have become so powerful if it wasn't? My five years were almost up. Couldn't they turn a blind eye the last month or two? Of course, while grappling with these questions, I had researched it myself when I had a free moment. It was indeed true. My work seemed done. I had to manage somehow. Somehow I managed to protect myself and stay in my room.

From work I was on sick leave from the salon for a week or two. Of course, unbeknownst to my brother-in-law and aunt, I got a report from the doctor. In the meantime, I could attend to my affairs. Because otherwise I didn't have time, since I worked five days in the hairdressing salon; from morning to night. Everywhere I went, my brother-in-law decided, even if it was a purchase, I had to let him know. He scared us. It was really hard living in fear.

In order not to be seen until the evening, I had to hide well from them. My first job was: I had to go to court and take custody of my siblings that my aunt gave me. I asserted that no one should have rights to my siblings. So I waited like everyone else for my turn. When it was my turn I told the lady there what she needed to know.

"Are you being beaten, violent attack, are the guardians addicted to alcohol or drugs? Why do you want to take care of them? Unless there are reasons I have listed, we cannot give you custody, the law is."

I was stunned by that. "There's violence at home, he's hitting my aunt!" I replied.

"Then have your aunt come and complain. If we get a record of her complaint, you will be granted custody."

"My aunt is afraid she won't complain about him," I said.

"I can't do anything for sir at the moment!" she said. As she was about to send me away, I quickly asked, "What if he's sexually harassing me?" The woman stared at me, wide-eyed! At that moment she put everything aside and gave me her full attention. "Do you take care of your siblings? Where are your parents?" she asked. I had tried to explain everything in my German that I had learned. Now I was talking and I wasn't scared at all. I wasn't worried that they would laugh at me or anything. So what she really wanted to ask was something else entirely.

The tough woman from earlier had turned into a kind and compassionate woman. "Do you know what that building is?"

"Yes, we're at the district attorney's office," I said confidently.

"You just said you were molested and you take responsibility for your siblings too. Since your siblings are minors. In this case, since it is a crime, the state does not ignore this crime but intervenes (for the sake of the children). That is the law of the state. Just as there is a mother's right and a father's right, the state takes care of us. I want you to testify. You may not be ready right now but the ability to at least put it on record when you file a criminal complaint will save you in this situation. One second; I'll make two phone calls and then I'll tell you what's going to happen."

The woman made plans for me. However, I was in shock and unable to file a criminal complaint because I was thinking of a quiet exit...I really don't want an exit like that.

While I was waiting for her, she phoned. As she hung up, she turned to me: "Now two police officers are coming, I don't want you to be scared. Calm down, relax. This will not be a criminal complaint. They record your statement and create a protocol. Otherwise, the state will press charges and take your siblings away from you. After submitting the statement, come back to me and let us fill out our written work and send our application as a petition so that we can take care of you. It's your choice…" she explained.

Another shock! "What did she say?" I couldn't believe what I was hearing. She officially said either your siblings or your statement. Actually, my answer was obvious. It was time to testify and apply for custody. So I said yes immediately. She was delighted.

After I filled out my statement, she gave it to the police officers. There was no letter from the public prosecutor's office to lodge a complaint. It means that the woman hadn't lied to me... I was very scared of that for the first few days because I didn't want them to know what I was dealing with. It had to remain hidden from them. I contacted Türkiye via the internet at an internet cafe until the rest of my break. My contacts sent me all the information and all the photos taken. She was under constant surveillance. But she wasn't even aware of it. Our famous dear Nalan lady! So I found out that she was still in a relationship with our family-friendly lawyer friend. It meant that their secret love is still ongoing.

My revenge began!

Still my brother Nihat was unaware of the situation. Who knows how many more schemes they had plotted against my brother. He was unaware of the danger. His accounts didn't look good either. They had peeled him like an onion.

Those were my first goals in Türkiye. First I wanted to wake up my brother. I owned all the pictures and had to send them to him somehow. He had to wake up from his deep sleep. This is how my revenge began. It was time, but I was in no hurry. One by one, my goals came naturally to me. So I felt very comfortable.

As a precaution, I kept my email address and ID number secret and sent the pictures to my brother - first to wake him up from his sleep. I sent him no notes, only pictures. They were photos of Mr. Lawyer and his affair with Nalân, showing very close, warm and friendly poses!

I was very curious about his reaction. But even though I sent them to him, they were still together. My brother hadn't even had those photos checked. Somehow Ms. Nalân had deceived my brother with her lies and hypocrisy. There was no other explanation for the fact that they were still together.

Sooner or later!
He'll serve every penalty!

Yasemin's Struggle

CHAPTER
27

I texted Nurgül while I was on sick leave. She had mentioned that at the beginning of the book. I wanted to open up to her and tell her that I was in danger, that I wasn't comfortable with my aunt, that I had two siblings and all the negative and positive memories I was harboring. She was the person I warmed to and my blood boiled with. My only, my merciful, my beautiful... My beautiful with a beautiful heart. Who had forgotten her own life, for she was her brother's soul. Because I wasn't going to work, she was very curious to know how I was doing. Since no one had thought of me until that day, it felt good that someone did. It was the first time I felt that feeling and I owed her my gratitude. It played a part in my short life but that short time encompassed all my years.

Another day out of the days;

Again my aunt had a date. My brother-in-law wasn't at home. Who knows what part of the world he found himself in again.

My siblings and I were at home in the evening... I was in a hurry and preparing the house. By now my siblings had washed up, after which they did their daily chores. They did the clothes, laundry, dishes... These were the duties of a housewife... I had a little trouble explaining human existence. We wouldn't always be perfect. After all, we all made mistakes.

In the midst of my rush, the outer door suddenly opened. At that moment I jumped up like crazy. My brother-in-law was standing in front of us. I froze in shock and covered my mouth with my hands. It was obvious I was scared. At that time, my brother-in-law stood in front of me and bit his lip with his teeth. I quickly retired to our room with my siblings.

Half an hour later, my brother-in-law called me, then he called again. But I ignored it. Suddenly he came closer, his voice getting closer and closer. He had called six or seven times. "Sister, my brother-in-law is calling you, answer him. You know it gets bad when he gets angry," Suat told me.

In a panic, I made a hand signal to Suat. "Okay, okay, please be quiet," I whispered, sensing the danger. Now he stood in front of the door, knocked loudly three times and called again: "Yasemin?"

By widening my eyes, I showed Suat that I was scared. "Please," I begged. Then I held Suat's hand and bent my face forward as if to cry. 'My God, please help us, I seek refuge in You, my fair lord. We have no refuge, no protector but You. Protect us from the people who oppress us, O Lord,' I prayed, taking refuge in God with tears streaming from my eyes.

At that moment, Suat said to me, "I'm with you too, sister, of course. There is, of course, God first. But please don't forget me, because I'm not little Suat anymore. If he raises his hand, then you have a brother who can protect you. I will never again let anyone raise their hand just so you know!"

I loved what he said. I felt honored, I hugged my brother. He felt old enough to protect his sister. It was an honorable feeling. But he didn't know; that his intention was not to raise his hand against me but to sexually harass me. How should I say the Suat? I couldn't pronounce it...

He called again, more tensely.

"Yasemin! I just called you said please, you still haven't come. What are you staying in your room for? Come here!"

"Go!" Suat asked me. I got up immediately and went to my brother-in-law.

"Please, did you want something?" I asked.

"Yes, I wanted something. Come on, fill the tub for me, but hot and sudsy. Get my towel and everything, I'm going for a swim," he demanded with a grin.

After I was done, I went back to my room. From time to time I had to look at the running water. When I saw the tub was full, I leaned over the tub to turn it off. At that moment, my brother-in-law leaned over me right behind me. "I wanted to take the temperature of the water," he lied. The weight of his whole body was on my back. With the other hand he held my waist for a second!

Suddenly I jerked up and pushed him away from me. He immediately grabbed my chin with one hand and my hand with the other and pushed me towards the washing machine with his whole body. I was motionless. But I didn't want to make a sound or my siblings would have heard. What Suat said went through my head. If I screamed now, he would even hit Suat because he wanted to defend me. In order not to put my brother in such a situation, I silently intervened.

I fought my brother-in-law with all my might, but he was well built. Suddenly he started kissing me while I was still trying to push him. He held my hand and with the other I pushed his head away from me to get rid of him. Everything as quiet as possible. A faint struggle could be heard, but he still hadn't realized the situation I was in.

When I went to the bathroom, Suat had retired to his room. Kiraz was alone in our room, lying in bed. He started rubbing my chest with his free hand while I was still pushing his head away with one hand. At that time, I managed to escape from his grasp by making a great effort. I ran to my room and locked my door. I was helpless and cried because I was afraid that he would break down the door and enter the room. My heart was beating like it was about to explode. No sound came from him. I wandered helplessly through my room, unable to stop for fear.

I was just very angry with Suat. *Why had he gone to his own room?* Now my thoughts were with him and I prayed that he had locked his door. I tried hard to hear and listen to him from the door, afraid he would do something to Suat. I quickly picked up my phone and left a message on my aunt's cell phone: "Come home quickly, and when you arrive, send Suat to our room immediately!"

Suddenly I overheard my brother-in-law and Suat chatting while I was texting Nurgül. I was so excited that I had sent it off halfway through, as my hand accidentally got on the button. But Suat was in great danger. I couldn't take it and opened the door. "Hey, what are you talking about?" I asked. Suat answered straight away, confused: "Just like that, from school and such." I quickly brought Suat to our room. Luckily I had made it and mustered all the courage. Now I was relieved and hugged him. "Until we leave this house, please don't sleep alone in your room," I demanded. Instantly, Suat realized something was wrong. "Let's go to bed, we're leaving in the morning," I said to Suat.

As soon as we were in bed, Suat fell asleep. My eyes were open until my aunt came and then until she fell asleep! In the meantime, Nurgül had left me a few messages.

"Who is it, Yasemin, who can enter the room? What happens there? If you're in danger, just say so!" She approached with a benevolent heart. So I texted her, "We'll be there in the morning," then put the phone down. At that time calls came from a withheld number. It was definitely my brother-in-law.

In the morning I left the house before six o'clock. Nurgül was very worried. She had prepared the lunch boxes for my siblings that morning. I hesitantly told her a little bit about what I had been through, but I couldn't put my finger on the situation. Because it had a different history. The ending of the film, which is not seen, is not clear.

At that moment, while going through my own pain, I was at Nurgül's home. As someone who respects privacy very much, she trusted me. Like a sister, she hugged me lovingly. As always, her attention was on me. As I spoke, she paid no attention to anything else. We didn't stay with her long, we left immediately as I had to take my siblings to school. So there was a hasty farewell.

The letter from the prosecutor was supposed to be sent to my place of work, but there was no news yet. Now I was getting impatient because I wanted to get out of there as soon as possible. Every day I stood in front of the prosecutor's office. But somehow I didn't get any results for my application.

It was unbearable, how had I gotten into such a state! *"Why do I have to wait five years, whose spirit will hear if I rent an apartment for the last few months?"* I thought for a while, because I've been in this house long enough.

At eight o'clock in the evening there was a knock on our door and we were all surprised. *I wonder who could that be? The first thing that came to mind was, could it be someone from the DA's office?* I approached the door. Suat rushed to open the door. When my brother-in-law saw me walking towards the door, he grabbed my shoulders. "Get out of my sight!" he snapped at me. I quickly moved a little away from the door without protesting. After Suat, my brother-in-law went to the door. My employer, colleague and Nurgül had come. I immediately put my hand over my mouth and prayed they wouldn't mess it up. People back home didn't know I was on sick leave, if that ever got out I was screwed.

When my brother-in-law returned with a bouquet in hand, he raised an eyebrow and with a slight smile said, "Here, these flowers are yours." As he handed me the flower, he gently palmed it across my chest glide as if he were caressing my chest.

He caught me again, I was negatively surprised at what had happened. Roughly I took the flowers in my hand and retreated to my room.

The camel's back was over. This time, this behavior had annoyed me more than usual. In my room, I mumbled to myself. In the meantime, my brother-in-law had once again taken my mobile phone from me for other reasons. He sensed I had a boyfriend so he took my phone away but left it off.

Another night was over. There was stale bread in the kitchen and I wanted to bake it for us because Suat likes fried eggs with bread. Also, I thought the kids would be able to take it to school tomorrow. So I cracked one egg at a time and added some spices. I toasted the egg rolls in the stove while I was deep in thought at work. It was nine thirty as far as I remembered.

By now I had toasted a whole tray of bread and had to make a pan of fried eggs. Halfway through my work, my brother-in-law walked into the kitchen, "What's your appetite this evening?" His mind was elsewhere again, that was obvious in every way. And what question did he ask? I got angry again. *But then I thought it won't be long, be patient. Have patience until the day you go.*

"Your aunt fell asleep on the sofa. Go on, cover her with something!" he urged me. I was surprised at that... Even though it was his wife, he couldn't even put a blanket over her. What a strange man my brother-in-law was! I quickly pulled the pan aside and went and threw a blanket over my aunt. When I came back, my brother-in-law was boiling water, apparently he wanted to drink tea. I was uncomfortable that he was in the kitchen, but I had work to do, the fries weren't ready yet. So I went back to the stove and got the fries ready.

My brother-in-law came a little closer to me, while he watched me. Of course I felt very bad. *Why is he looking at me,* I kept muttering to myself. Then he grabbed the closet door hanging on the wall right next to me. He stretched extra so that I found myself between his two arms and his body. I had to bend down to get out of there. Just as I was about to push him away, he took a few steps back.

"OK! OK! Calm down, watch your voice, you'll wake up the others," he whispered softly, making hand signals. There we had had a face-to-face conversation on this topic for the first time, so that no one heard. He didn't seem to mind. After cleaning up the kitchen, I retired to my room. I lay on my bed with my eyes open until I couldn't hear anything from inside.

The next morning my brother-in-law said goodbye to all of us and was away again for a few days. My aunt had a very important doctor's appointment. She certainly wouldn't be home before noon. My sick note lasted anyway. Although this was an opportunity, I didn't have to go out, nobody was home. After taking my siblings to school, I came home. First I had a quiet breakfast, then I cleaned up and vacuumed the floor. While I was changing the garbage bags, I heard someone enter the apartment. I froze on the spot because I was shocked and very scared.

Who had come? I couldn't go to the kitchen door for fear. Suddenly my brother-in-law was standing in the kitchen door and staring at me.

What was he doing at home? Surely he thought the same about me. He slowly entered the kitchen and asked me questions. The garbage bags in my hand rustled as my hands trembled with fear.

"Brother-in-law, why did you come home?" I asked, horrified.

"What about you?" he asked a counter-question.

"I got sick at work, they sent me home," I stammered.

"Then lie down instead of working at home, come on, put things out of your hands," he urged me.

He immediately took the bag from my hand and put it on the counter with his other hand, but he didn't give me the way so I could go through. There were kitchen cabinets on one side and a dining table and chairs on the other. I went left and right to get past him but he didn't budge.

In a split second he grabbed my hair from behind, reached over my shoulders and began caressing my chest and kissing my neck. When he pulled my hair from behind, my neck felt freer. I pushed him away with one hand, kicking him with my feet as much as I could. With my free hand, I slapped his arm, his shoulder, his back, his face, his head, anywhere I could get my hands on it. Escape was impossible, but I kept kicking and punching him to get away from him. Then he held my hand and pushed me towards the kitchen cabinets and leaned against me, his full body weight on me.

"Let go, stop it!" I yelled at him. But it was in vain, he did not stop. Somehow he had managed to make me motionless. He pushed himself violently between my legs. With one hand he held my hands overhead and with the other he was still gripping my breasts.

"Let it go, let go of me!" I shrieked, but he covered my mouth. He was over me, doing his best to immobilize me.

I kept screaming, "Don't do it, don't!"

Suddenly the house phone rang. The sudden noise had distracted him. Finally I was able to escape by pushing him away with my arms and all my strength.

There was a large, long knife on the counter, which I immediately grabbed. I held the knife in one hand and made a fist with the other.

"If you touch me again with your hand and your body, I'll cut you into pieces, do you understand me? I will chop you up! I have nothing to lose. I'll cut you into pieces, do you understand me?" I yelled, my hands and legs shaking.

Only God knows how I got out of the apartment because I don't remember anymore. I soon found myself with the police because I wanted to file a criminal complaint. Now I could prove it, because I had traces of his beatings on my body.

He had banged my head against the wall several times, he bit my arm, and bruises from his grip on my arms were left.

I had emphatically insisted that my siblings be withdrawn from school. I had done everything to keep them from going home. After I had my siblings with me, I wanted to stop by the salon. Because I didn't have a phone anymore, which he had taken from me, I couldn't even call. I had an appointment with Nurgül that morning. It was almost noon now. As soon as I got out of the police car and entered the salon, they all rushed me. They really all hugged me.

"I left home, Nurgül, are you coming with me?" I asked her. I was nervous, scared and exhausted.

The only one I trusted was Nurgül. Now I had no one but her and my siblings. When our boss gave her approval, we took Nurgül and returned to the police station with my siblings and the police.

Nurgül was very surprised. She couldn't ask me right away but at every opportunity she asked: "What happened to you, Yasemin? don't be silent! Tell me!"

The police said they would take me to a women's shelter with my siblings. Suddenly my feet felt strange in the corridor of the police station, I got dizzy. It was like pouring boiling water over me, then I passed out. When I came to, I was in a hospital room. "You had a nervous breakdown," the doctors said.

Foam had come out of my mouth, my eyes had been white. I couldn't remember that. After I regained consciousness, I wanted to leave the hospital immediately. I wanted to get out of town as soon as possible. It was like running away from danger! Once the doctors measured my blood pressure, there was nothing stopping me from leaving the hospital.

In the evening, it was already after seven, the police escorted my siblings and me to a women's shelter.

We stayed in the women's shelter for three days. The local officials/social workers found us an apartment in a remote location very quickly, found me a job and registered my siblings at school. Since they knew that we came from the women's shelter, my siblings were immediately accepted at school without any problems. We had looked at the apartment, spoken to the landlord and signed our mutual agreement. I loved the apartment right away, my heart felt warm at first sight. It was my first home. I looked at my first home with a lot of love. It was the metropolis we would live in. It would be a fresh start for us.

If life is full of wars,
man's weapon is in his soul!

CHAPTER
28

Here the state had taken care of us. It was the only refugee state. After running away from my relatives, the state took me under its protection. I don't regret that I came to Germany. Yes, I had experienced five years of agony. From the day I arrived until this day I had suffered. What would you say now maybe right, maybe it was wrong? Who knows? But I only understood one thing, Germany was a country that does not disregard human rights, and therefore, as an affected woman, I felt safe in this country.

"You can move into the apartment at the beginning of the month," he said, but since our situation was urgent, the landlord let us move into the apartment immediately. I had to start from scratch, because I had siblings I had to be even stronger from now on. We called Nurgül and communicated with each other. They came to my house with the whole salon team. I remembered that day well. I had also bought a lot of furniture at a reduced price from the state.

In the first phase I saw a lot of help from the state. Then I looked at my apartment today, "mashallah", nothing was missing in our apartment. We had a fully furnished apartment and there was even an idyllic garden. Thank you God ...

I secretly called my aunt. "What day does my brother-in-law return home?" I asked.

"He left yesterday, he won't be home for five days. So he returns after three days, why do you ask? Where are you, Yasemin?"

"Do us a favor anyway. Pack everything we have in our rooms. Pack our clothes in our suitcases and all the odds and ends in boxes. Please, aunt," I begged.

"Okay, my child, okay. I will do it. What happened? Yasemin, did your brother-in-law do something to you? Where will you stay now?" she asked.

"I'm still unable to answer you. My only request to you is; Gathering up all our stuff, everything... I'll be there tomorrow night at 8 o'clock. Please get everything ready by this hour, we don't want anything more there," I said.

This was a new excitement for me. I had to go to my aunt's to get our stuff, that was a must. That day I went by train, my siblings stayed at home alone. My employer and Nurgül also came to my aunt to help me. After that, they would drop me off at my apartment with my belongings. We were able to pick up our things from my aunt without a hitch. I was very relieved about that. It was my personal property.

It was pretty late. After sending my siblings to bed, I looked for the wooden box in the packages. All my favorite pieces were in there, they meant a lot to me. A large amount of money that I received from my brother was also in the box. I didn't know how much was in the envelope. The pictures and everything that reminded me of my good times were in my box. Only I had the key.

I lovingly opened the box and was lost in the old days. From time to time I would burst into sobs, and from time to time I would reminisce and smile a little.

I think Nurgül wrote the rest at the very beginning. This is what I had been through. Not once had I spoken about the negative events I had experienced, there were some I didn't share, but most of them did by the time I got to the end of my audio recordings? Maybe. Maybe I was really at the end now.

Another memory just came to mind. I recently had a phone conversation with Nurgül. She told me that she had started writing down my notes. I was very happy about that but also excited. She told me about her work without going into the content of the audio recordings I sent.

"When you talk about the book. What do you think it should be called?" she asked me. It was an unexpected question, it hadn't occurred to me. Realizing I was having trouble answering, Nurgül felt very confident.

"YASEMIN'S STRUGGLE" she said smiling slightly. With admiration and surprise I replied, "What?" I smiled very confidently.

"Yes, Yasemin's struggle," I said. It was amazing, I loved the title of the book. *Nurgül had a strong sense and writing skills. If she said so, so be it.* This is how the book title came about. Now I was at the end of my audio recording..."

Now Yasemin had finished her recordings. And I devoted my time to writing a book. When we spoke on the phone from time to time, we always talked about our intensity.

At first I didn't tell Yasemin so that she wouldn't get upset, but her brother-in-law looked for her and asked me with a smile to reveal Yasemin's whereabouts. A few times he was in the front door of my workplace or sometimes he blocked my way during the break. Each time I replied, "I don't know!" However, he didn't believe me. He never believed it...

When I started to sense danger, I couldn't take it anymore. So I told Yasemin everything. I hadn't heard from her since then. She even changed her phone number.

About a month had passed. I still hadn't heard any news. So I wrote her a letter and sent it. Four and a half weeks later my letter came back...

God, I started to falter. I asked my employer: "What do you say, should we go to Yasemin's in the next few days? She cannot be reached by phone and the letter I wrote was returned to me. I'm worried."

"Of course we'll go there tomorrow night," my boss promised.

When we looked at her house, we saw that Yasemin no longer lived there. She was gone... gone without a trace. There were no clues. She flew out of my hand, Yasemin...

Later I regretted it very much. I was so angry with myself that I wished I had never been approached by her brother-in-law, maybe then she wouldn't have cut off contact with me.

But something happened, in whatever direction. You had to wish the best for everything.

It doesn't matter if he's in his life or
in a work environment.
If a relationship doesn't make you happy, let it go.

Yasemin's Struggle

CHAPTER
29

Eight years later!

I spent almost every spare minute working on the book. With two jobs, housekeeping, etc., I didn't have much time to spare and only wrote occasionally. My work went on like this for a year and a half, and then I had decided to finish the book. Now I had to find a publisher.

I was scammed by several publishers. Therefore, the printing was delayed again and again.

Because of my dealings with publishers, my time on the book grew longer by the day.

After I wrote this book, I put it in a little box.

I read it every now and then as I recalled those days and as I read I gained new insights and remembered Yasemin.

I hadn't heard from Yasemin for eight years. Out of sight but not out of my heart. *Who knows where she was now?*

Eight years later, a sign of life came from Yasemin via Facebook. She wrote a message from her fake profile. I was over the moon about that, at least I hoped she was. She sent me an invitation to speak on camera. To protect myself, I had turned off my own camera, but it really was Yasemin. She had changed a lot. How happy I was when I saw her.

"I'm on my way to Frankfurt, but I didn't want to continue without stopping by," she said. The world had been mine. I agreed to a meeting on the spot. I was very happy about her message.

We wanted to meet in an hour and a half, after eight years. You can't imagine how I spent that hour and a half. I was at the peak of joy and excitement. I hurriedly went to the address where we wanted to meet. As soon as I sat down, Yasemin came.

"What a beautiful place, reminiscent of the highlands," were her first words. We hugged sincerely... Then, when we both sat happily in our seats, holding each other with one hand, she said, "Congratulations on your book, Nurgül!" I thanked her and told her that the publishers had cheated that I worked hard, put in a lot of effort, but lost my enthusiasm for my daily positive and negative activities. In a very understanding way, she said, "I see." Her hand was still on mine.

Yasemin had completely changed her image. A businesswoman was standing in front of me. A wonderful sight, my beautiful Yasemin. "Maybe after our meeting today it will motivate me and I can finish my work. May I see and meet you again?" I asked, smiling. She was delighted, her hopeful blue eyes smiling at me.

In a hurry, Yasemin said to me, "I can't stay more than fifteen minutes. I have to continue on my way. You are successful, I follow you even if you don't know it. Even if I don't know everything, I know that you've been through a lot. You're exhausted, what made you sad or tired?" she asked. I didn't want to go into those things, in fact we only had fifteen minutes and it had already been five minutes.

I was hoping so much that she would leave me her phone number or contact information. However, Yasemin tried to explain that she couldn't give me contact information because she didn't want to get me into trouble. It would be better that way because she was thinking of me because she didn't want me to get hurt.

What damage? What was Yasemin talking about? Was she in danger? It was eating me up inside. This meeting had made me very thoughtful. She hadn't even told me what city she lived in. How likely was it that something like this would happen.

The time to say goodbye was near. The meeting was very short and we still had so much to tell each other... "It is necessary to let the passenger go freely on the way, says a Turkish proverb.

Sorry, Nurgül," she regretted, standing up and approaching a hug. After kissing and hugging me, she suddenly dropped a voice recorder assistant into my hand. Inside was a cassette.

I stared at Yasemin in shock. She walked away without looking back. I stared after her until she was out of sight. The excitement was at its peak. Thousands of questions ran through my mind but she was gone.

Before I left I wanted to pay the bill and called the waiter. "Paid!" he replied in monosyllables. The whole time she never took her eyes off me. On the way to my apartment, I thought about how she could pay the bill in the blink of an eye.

I wanted to hear Yasemin's audio recording as soon as possible. So I prepared everything and devoted my full attention to the cassette.

"A lot has changed in my life since we met and since we haven't seen each other. Unpredictable changes have occurred. My siblings are still with me and they will stay with me as long as they want, God willing. I never gave up and I am the same Yasemin today as I used to be. Kiraz is doing her high school diploma to prepare for university. Suat is a model boy. He graduated from high school as the second best with honors and is now studying. I hope that he completes his studies just as successfully. It's almost time, I'm patient. After my vocational training, I enrolled in the master school and successfully received my master's certificate. Now I run three salons, all three are mine. But we work day and night. This is the first information about us that happened in the 8 years ...

But a lot has accumulated in these eight years. Many things have changed in my life. As I chronicled my past experiences, I was able to digest everything and my eyes were opened. I feel an improvement in myself and at the same time a relief. I can say it felt like therapy. Talking is really relaxing. It's good that you told me then that I should talk. This record will be very short. When I have time, I would like to start recording again and send you audio recordings. That's why I left you this recording assistant after I said goodbye.

Yasemin ended her struggle; looking for revenge... Yasemin gradually began to take revenge during these eight years. I'm in no hurry, I'll have all the bills paid one at a time very soon. "

"I STAND ABOVE MY STRUGGLE. NOW IS TIME FOR REVENGE!!!"

Yasemin ended her recording with these words:

"I survived my struggle, now it's time for revenge."

That means **YASEMINS REVENGE 3** awaits us.

Let's wait ...

The End

READER COMMENTS

Hello Nurgül, today I saw the cover of your second book. I follow your site and have seen that people can share their opinions with you after reading your books. I also wanted to write something about this because the topic you wrote really includes today›s problems. It must be read and shared because this book is proof of how strong a human being can be. Sometimes I say: if all this evil could be wiped out of this world if only the good remained, but I know it›s impossible. I hope that one day all the bad things will be corrected and all the Yasemins will be happy.

ANONYM

Hello Sister Nurgül, I congratulate you from the bottom of my heart. I have read both books. Did Yasemin really experience all this? It›s so hard to believe if it were me, I would be either a murderer or a victim awaiting death. I›m glad you wrote these books. I hope they give someone hope. I believe it will be so! I am glad to know you. I love you.

Ecem DÖNMEZ

Hello Nurgül, I have read your two books. I congratulate you. After I finished this book, I really wanted to meet Yasemin. She really is a strong and courageous person. Not everyone could handle that. Congratulations on your writing. I will eagerly await your new books.

ANONYM

Dear dear Mrs. Nurgül. I am a member of the women's charity. I have read your book with great admiration. I would like to speak to you privately about your book. However your time allows. We can realize beautiful and positive projects around your book. We can realize the project of my idea as a team with the members of the women's industry solidarity platform. As a team, we stand behind you in your announcement to say no to violence against women and not to remain silent. May your success keep rising higher and higher. Kind regards.

ANONYM

A cruel life! I finished Yasemin›s struggle. My heart was torn. I made it my duty to read it, because you feel it is your duty to make that voice heard by thousands. Cover photos are perfectly coherent, match the cover and carefully selected, editing and proofreading available, quality is perfect. Congratulations, it›s a job well done.

ANONYM

Dear Ms. Nurgül, I finally found you on social media. I focused on Yasemin›s series. Put my work aside and found myself right on topic. Real life was my area of interest. The book exceeded my expectations. It was a quick read but still has an impact. Will there be series three? What is Yasemin›s real name? Is she still talking to you? Thank you for publishing an interesting book. May your writing attain success after success.

ANONYM

Hi. I wanted to write to you about your books. I can say it is one of the best books I have ever read. I usually prefer to read books about real life, which has always fascinated me. In fact, every time I buy a book, I have absolute hesitation, but then I›m satisfied and I see the books I use as nighttime reading increase. That›s exactly what happened in both of your books. I finished the first book in one breath and immediately picked up the second book and it was done in one breath. Writing like this requires solid psychology and experience. As far as I can see this is all available to you. I congratulate you very much. I hope you always write the truth. With love.

ANONYM

Hello dear Nurgül, I have read your two books. I want to congratulate you on the topic you have chosen. It takes great courage to write these books. Above all, I congratulate you on your courage and ambition. I hope that with this book everything you set out to do will come true. Regards.

Nuran ALAGÖZ

Matilda Türkçe

Savaşın İçinden Bir Kelebek

Sert Kapak - İnce Kapak - e-kitap

Matilda Deutsch

Ein Schmetterling inmitten des Krieges

Paperback - Hardcover - e-book

Matilda English

A butterfly through the war

Paperback - Hardcover - e-book

 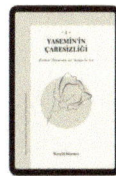

Yasemin'in Çaresizliği - 1 Türkçe

Binlerce Yasemin'den Bir Yasemin'in Sesi

Sert Kapak - İnce Kapak - e-kitap

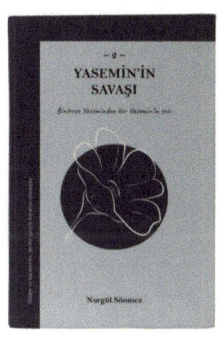 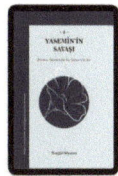

Yasemin'in Savaşı - 2 Türkçe

Binlerce Yasemin'den Bir Yasemin'in Sesi

Sert Kapak - İnce Kapak - e-kitap

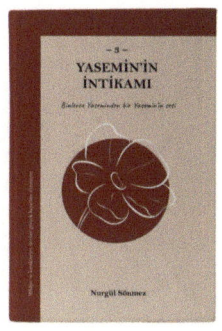 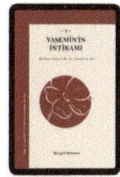

Yasemin'in İntikamı - 3 Türkçe

Binlerce Yasemin'den Bir Yasemin'in Sesi

Sert Kapak - İnce Kapak - e-kitap

Yasemins Verzweiflung - 1 Deutsch

Eine Stimme unter Tausenden

Paperback - Hardcover - e-book

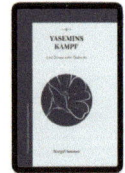

Yasemins Kampf - 2 Deutsch

Eine Stimme unter Tausenden

Paperback - Hardcover - e-book

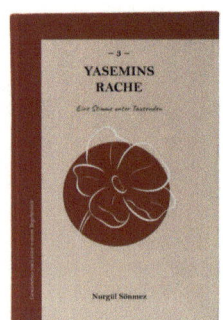

Yasemins Rache - 3 Deutsch

Eine Stimme unter Tausenden

Paperback - Hardcover - e-book

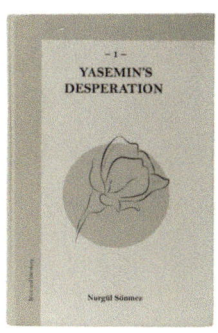
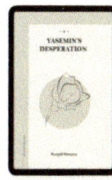

Yasemins Desperation - 1 English

One voice among thousands

Paperback - Hardcover - e-book

Yasemins Struggle - 2 English

One voice among thousands

Paperback - Hardcover - e-book

Yasemins Revenge - 3 English

One voice among thousands

Paperback - Hardcover - e-book

1001 Gece Yerine Bin Bir Gün Türkçe

"Özgürlüğe süzülen bir mülteci"

Sert Kapak - İnce Kapak - e-kitap

Statt 1001 Nacht - Tausendundein Tag Deutsch

"Weg in die Freiheit"

Paperback - Hardcover - e-book

Instead Of 1001 Night – One Thousand and One Day English

"A refugee soaring to freedom"

Paperback - Hardcover - e-book

Maarouf Türkçe

"Vatanı tarafından terk edilmiş bir adamın, inanılmaz öyküsü"

Sert Kapak - İnce Kapak - e-kitap

Maarouf Deutsch

"Ein Mann, der von seiner Heimat verlassen wurde"

Paperback - Hardcover - e-book

Maarouf English

"The incredible story of a man abandoned his homeland by force"

Paperback - Hardcover - e-book

■ **Sunduğumuz hizmetler:**

Almanca, İngilizce, Fransızca ve Türkçe dillerinde uzman edebi kitap çevirileri.

• Editörlük - Almanca, İngilizce, Fransızca, Türkçe
• Düzeltme - Almanca, İngilizce, Fransızca, Türkçe

Siz de eser(ler)inizin çevirisini yapmak ve ek hizmetlerimizden (redaksiyon, düzenleme, kitap kapağı tasarımı, illüstrasyon & kitap dizgisi) yararlanmak istiyorsanız bize ulaşın.

➤ Talebinizi bize e-posta ile gönderebilirsiniz.

■ **Nous offrons:**

Des traductions littéraires professionnelle des livre en allemand, anglais, française et turc.

• Lectorat - Allemand, Anglais, Français, Turc
• Lecture de correction - Allemand, Anglais, Français, Turc

Vous êtes également intéressé par la traduction littéraire de votre ou vos œuvres et par le bénéfice de nos services complémentaires (relecture, correction, conception de couvertures de livres, illustration et composition de livres).

➤ Alors envoyez-nous votre demande par e-mail.

■ **Wir bieten:**

In den Sprachen Deutsch, Englisch, Türkisch und Französisch fachgerechte literarische Buchübersetzung an. Zusätzlich;

• Lektorat - Deutsch, Englisch, Türkisch, Französisch
• Korrekturlesen - Deutsch, Englisch, Türkisch, Französisch

Sie haben auch Interesse Ihr Werk oder Ihre Werke literarisch zu Übersetzen und von unseren zusätzlichen Dienstleistungen zu profitieren (Lektorat, Korrekturlesen, Buchcover Design, Illustration & Buchsatz).

▷ Dann schicken Sie uns Ihre Anfrage per Email.

■ **We offer:**

Professional literary book translation in German, English, Turkish and French.

• Editing - German, English, Turkish, French
• Droofreading - German, English, Turkish, French

You are also interested in literary translation of your work(s) and benefit from our additional services (Editing, droofreading, book cover design, illustration & book typesetting).

▷ Then send us your request by email.